YOU REALLY LIKED THAT?

STORIES FROM PULPHOUSE FICTION MAGAZINE

Edited by
DEAN WESLEY SMITH

You Really Liked That?

Published by WMG Publishing Inc.
Cover and interior design copyright © 2019 WMG Publishing Inc.
Cover art copyright © 2019 by interactimages / Depositphotos
ISBN-13: 978-1-56146-078-6
ISBN-10: 1-56146-078-8

CONTENTS

INTRODUCTION

At my desk I have many notebooks and slips of paper. One small notebook was dedicated for putting this book together and nothing more. I kept track over the last year of any good comments I heard or got about any story in the first year, plus Issue Zero of *Pulphouse Fiction Magazine*.

Let me stress the word "good." Honestly I got no bad comments about any story. More than likely I would not have, since I am the editor. But wow did I get a lot of great comments.

Far more than I had hoped when I started my notebook to keep track.

Some of the comments I passed on to the author, but most of the time I just wrote the name of the story in that small notebook.

Normally, to do a book like this, we would send out to readers some sort of poll. Now that kind of reader survey works great in an established magazine when the poll has been sent out year after year. Those reader polls have value to not only the magazine, but to the authors who have stories selected.

But this is our first year at *Pulphouse Fiction Magazine* and if we had sent out such a poll, it would have been answered mostly by people who like answering polls (yes there are people like that, shockingly enough) and authors. Such a poll would not have been a good representation of reader feelings about the stories.

So right after Issue Zero came out in late 2017, I took it on myself to keep track of reader comments. They came at me in emails, usually as a "by the way, I really loved…"

They also came at me in personal conversations at conferences and I would make note of the comment. I also made note of comments on social media about a story. Those were often seconds or thirds of an original comment.

And I included comments in reviews. Amazing how many comments came when I opened my mind to hearing them.

The most commented on and liked story in my records was by Kent Patterson from Issue Zero. "Spud Wrangler" is about a stampede of Idaho baked potatoes and it flat beat out every other story by a long ways in comments from readers.

Kent had other stories on my list, but I am only going to put "Spud Wrangler" in this short book.

The second most mentioned and complimented story was Robert Jeschonek's story "In the Empire of Underpants" about a sentient pair of men's briefs. Robert also had other stories on my list, but again for room I am only putting in the one.

Annie Reed came in a close third with her wonderful story "Queen of the Mouse Riders" out of Issue #1.

From there, every story in this collection got numbers of positive comments. I had far too many stories on my list to put in this collection and honestly, as the editor of *Pulphouse Fiction Magazine,* that makes me very happy. It was wonderful over this first year to see readers reacting so positively to authors' work and to the magazine itself.

So thank you one and all, for the support initially in our first Kickstarter subscription drive and for staying with us over this first year and into our second year. We're having fun.

And I hope you enjoy this crazy group of stories from the first year of *Pulphouse Fiction Magazine.*

—Dean Wesley Smith
January 5th, 2019
Las Vegas, Nevada

SPUD WRANGLER

KENT PATTERSON

Kent Patterson was a polio survivor and one of the nicest and smartest men I have ever had the pleasure to meet. Those of you lucky enough to be young enough to not remember the polio epidemic and the vaccine that saved us, do go look it up. A nasty disease.

Kent's body was ravaged by his days with polio, yet it never seemed to slow him down. As one of the longest-lived survivors, Kent decided to take up fiction writing and he did it with his usual charm and wit and incredible drive.

Everyone who has read a Kent Patterson story has a different favorite. This is mine. I published it in issue #17 of the original Pulphouse Magazine *in 1994 and a short time later Kent finally lost his lifetime fight with polio. But during his short stint writing fiction, he had sold to* F&SF, Analog, Pulphouse, *and many other magazines.*

And thanks go to Jerry Oltion for doing the fantastic work of keeping Kent's wonderful stories in print and available after two decades.

———

With the suddenness of a rifle shot, a desert thunderclap rumbled and rolled across the Idaho plains. Here and there scattered rain drops fell, kicking up tiny puffs of dust where they hit the dry ground.

"That there were a close 'un," drawled old Parley McKonky. Clucking gently, he reined in his horse. "Now, now, there, there," he said, patting the horse's neck. "Just a little desert storm, and it ain't agoin' to eat you." The horse trembled, its nostrils flared and its eyes wide with fear.

Brig Clark's horse stood placidly as a cardboard cow. Couldn't even hear it thunder, Brig thought with disgust. Of course they always gave the oldest horse to the newest wrangler. A fourteen-year-old boy got treated nothing better than a baby when wranglers were concerned. He glanced at Parley. The old man's face was as wrinkled as a outcropping of lava. Hat off, head raised, he sniffed the air. So did his horse.

"Boy, there's trouble brewing." He looked at Brig. "You're going to earn a wrangler's pay today. That lightning hit close. Real close. Somewhere around Twin Missionaries Springs. Now tell me what you smell."

Brig sniffed. He smelled mostly horse, sage brush, and maybe a touch of grungy underwear. He took off his hat and tried again. There was something else. The musty scent of desert rain. And something else yet, a faint aroma which reminded him of his mother's kitchen.

"That's the smell a spud wrangler fears most, son." Parley gave him a keen glance. "That smell, son, is baked potato." He raised his hand for silence. "Put your ear to the ground, boy, and listen."

Brig climbed down from his horse. Holding the reins in one hand, he lay flat. Raindrops speckled the dirt with little brown craters. Brig placed his ear on the ground and strained to hear. He heard leather reins creaking, the hoarse breathing of his horse. A hoarse horse, he thought wildly.

Then he heard it. Not a sound, really, but a trembling in the ground.

"That's a stampede, son, and it's coming our way." Parley lit a cigarette, the smell of tobacco permeating the air. "They're coming our way, and they're coming hard. And there ain't one damned thing between them and Snake River Canyon but you and me."

An image of Snake River Canyon flashed through Brig's mind. You popped over a little ridge and there it was, a sheer cliff of black lava dropping four hundred feet straight down. He'd seen a horse fall off it once. Ants had eaten the remains. There wasn't a piece big enough to interest anything else.

"That herd's the entire year's crop." Parley looked at Brig. "If the panic spreads to the main herd, which it will if we don't stop it—," his voice dropped off. "Well, it'll be a mighty long, hungry winter in Idaho. We got maybe two hours."

"But I don't have a watch."

"Take a look at where the sun is," said Parley, pointing to the sun which just now burst out from behind the storm cloud. "See where it's going to hit Hanged Man Spike?" Brig looked. Hanged Man Spike was a lava outcropping that stabbed into the Western sky like a broken tooth. "By the time the sun hits the Spike, the herd will hit the Canyon."

"What we going to do?" Brig asked, ashamed at the quaver in his voice.

"We got us a few minutes to spare. I'm finishing my smoke. You, well, boy, if you got to go, you better go now. You might not get a better chance all day."

Brig looked around for a rest room, or even a tall bush. Nothing for miles except tumbleweeds, scanty patches of cheat grass, and knee high sage brush stretching off in all directions in rows as neatly as if it had been planted. He took a deep breath, unzipped, and peed standing in the open desert like a man, leaving a miniature Snake River Canyon in the dust.

He remounted his horse, pulled an Idaho Spud candy bar from his saddle bag, split the wrapper with a single thrust of his thumbnail like his daddy had taught him, and began to eat. The rich, chocolate marshmallow taste mixed with the flavor of horse and desert dust.

Now the air reeked with the smell of baked potato.

The ground trembled. Brig munched his candy bar. Control yourself, he told himself. Real wranglers don't sweat. He stole a glance at Parley, puffing his smoke calmly as if the stampede were a radio show on a station he couldn't get.

Now the trembling in the ground shook the air. Parley's horse pranced back and forth, rolling the whites of its eyes and sawing its mouth against the bit. Even Brig's horse lifted its head and whinnied, staring off to the north where a low ridge of lava blocked the view. "Finally something woke you up," Brig whispered to the horse. "I thought you was dead."

The rumbling became a roar. Now even Parley stared at the giant clouds of dust billowing up in the North. He glanced at Brig. "You ready, son?" he shouted over the roar.

Not trusting himself to speak, Brig nodded.

"Remember, boy. We're all there is between the herd and the canyon. We don't turn 'em, you know the only thing we'll need?"

A brown tidal wave of potatoes burst over the low lava ridge. A flood of Idaho Number One Bakers the size of bread loaves, tumbling end over end, eyes white with panic.

Parley's last few words died in the thunder of the stampede. But the joke was ancient, and Brig knew it well. If the herd went over the canyon wall, all a spud wrangler needed was five hundred tank cars of gravy.

"Ki yi yee yee, roll you bakers roll!" Parley shouted the traditional cry of the spud wrangler. His horse shot forward like a cannonball. Through the last of his candy bar, Brig tried shouting too, but his mouth was so dry he only succeeded in spraying himself with chocolate marshmallow and bits of coconut. He glanced at the hordes of potatoes now streaming through every gap in the lava ridge and rolling down the plain as irresistibly as Noah's flood. His horse whinnied in fear and, in spite of Brig tightening the reins, it shied backwards, away from the thunder of the onrushing spuds. "You're making a coward of me, horse," Brig said.

But it was him making a coward of himself. He whose sweaty hands slipped on the reins, whose breath came short, whose pulse pounded like Satan's own trip hammer in his brain. He tried to yell a "Ki yi yi" but the sound turned to dust and chocolate in his mouth.

Spur your horse, spur you coward, he screamed in his mind. But try as he might, his spurs seemed to have a will of their own. Unbidden, tears sprang to his eyes. Bless the Lord that Parley was halfway across the flat and couldn't see.

Turn back. Get out of here. For a second he decided to give the horse its head, race away from that implacable, thundering mass of spuds, get away and live.

But, even as his horse turned, an image flashed through his mind. The wranglers gathered around the chuck wagon after a hard day's work. Tired, aching, maybe hurt, but each knowing he'd done his share, that he'd never let a partner down. The Idaho sunset, turning the desert purple and pink, with maybe a single puff of cloud flaring gold in an empty sky. Night slipping across the desert plain, the camp fire crackling, smelling of sage. A couple of prime Idaho Number Ones turning on a spit, the comforting sound of male voices laughing, joking about big spuds and beautiful women.

If he turned away now, he would never be one of them. Oh, no one would say a thing. Not by a whisper, not by a hint, would anyone breathe the word "coward." No one would have to.

But in the morning when he woke up he'd find a potato peeler by his bed. There was nothing written down, but the rule was iron. Men herded spuds. Cowards were only fit for making french fries.

Brig closed his eyes. "Ki yi yee yee," he squeaked. He opened his eyes and shouted louder. "Ki yi yee yee." Louder yet! He spurred his horse. It shied. He spurred harder. "Ki yi yee yee!" he screamed at the top of his voice. "Roll on, you bakers." Hooves drummed on the dry desert dust as his horse headed for the rampaging herd of potatoes.

Minutes turned into hours, days, as Brig charged down the long lines of the potato herd. Screaming, shouting, waving his arms and brandishing his long black spud masher, he and Parley drove the huge lead spuds back. If these turned, the herd followed, rumbling along like a freight train. But sometimes the lead spuds resisted even the masher, and then Brig would resort to the spud wrangler's greatest and most ancient weapon, holding his arms overhead in the mystical half circle that for reasons unknown drove terror into the very starch of even the toughest tuber. That always worked, though no spud wrangler knew why.

Dust billowed high into the sky, the few sprinkles of rain long since dried out in the blazing summer sun. Brig pulled his bandanna over his nose and mouth. Dust covered him until he and his horse looked like some grey monster out of the past.

But the herd turned. Gradually, the lead spuds circled, sweeping their followers into a gigantic spud whirlpool. Hoarse with shouting, his face caked with dust, Brig felt like a hero, a genuine spud wrangler at last.

In the distance, he saw Parley riding up fast, waving his arms and yelling words lost in the thunder of the spud herds.

So what now, Brig thought. The work's nearly over. He couldn't make out what Parley was saying. "How we doing?" he shouted as Parley came up.

"Run for your life!" Parley shouted.

Only then did Brig notice the rumbling of the spud herds had taken on a deeper, throbbing, more menacing sound. He looked to the north. Over the ridge came a solid wall of bakers which blotted out the sky. Brig had never seen spuds panicked like that, climbing on top of each other to get away. He knew this could only be the main herd, the livelihood of half the state. It was a spud avalanche, a city of spuds set up on edge and stampeding across the Idaho plains. Parley streaked towards the high ground of Mormon Butte. Brig followed.

He didn't have to urge his horse to run. However old and

tired, she was a spud horse and knew all too well what that ground-shaking roar meant.

Brig didn't look back. He could sense that towering mass looming over him.

A shadow slipped over his head. The potato herd blocked out the sun. Now he was on the welcome slopes of Mormon Butte. Higher! He had to get higher up the slope to be safe, "Come on, old gal," he urged on his horse. "Just a few more steps." He glanced back as the great wave of potatoes crested high over his head. "Jump for your life!" he shouted, driving in his spurs. With one great convulsive heave, his horse leaped just as truckloads of spuds smashed down.

"Good horse, great horse!" She stood shivering, foam spuming down her flanks. High on Mormon Butte, they were safe for the moment. Brig watched the masses of spuds surging by. Thousands had been broken or mashed. The air reeked with hot starch. The horse's flanks rose and fell.

"Parley!" Brig shouted. Parley lay flat on the ground on his back. One hand held his horse's reins. Brig dismounted, leading his horse, and ran up to Parley.

Parley stared at the blank sky. One arm jutted out at an impossible angle. A trickle of blood ran from his mouth.

"Parley, you're hurt."

"Don't mind me, kid. Mind the herd."

"But there's too many of them."

Parley coughed, and stared at the sky. Then he spoke.

"They're scared, son. Just plain blind panicked. And a scared spud can't see beyond the sprouts of its eyes. It's barely an hour now till they hit Snake River Canyon. Take my horse. It's faster. You've got to stop them. Everything's up to you now." Parley turned his head.

"What do I do, Parley? How can I get them to turn?" He looked down at the ocean of spuds. Nothing could turn that herd.

"Only one way to turn a herd of scared spuds, son," Parley said. "Get there first and find something to scare them worse than the lightning did. Now git. Go."

Without a word, Brig mounted Parley's horse and spurred along Mormon Ridge. The ridge, he knew, ran southeast a couple of miles, then petered out. He had to flank the spuds, run along the ridge until he could get in front of them, then drop down to the plain. He glanced over his shoulder at the sun. Hanged Man's Spike nearly touched the round red disk.

He could get ahead of the spuds, but then what? How could a lone boy turn a herd that skunked even real wranglers? The horse's hoofbeats drummed in his head like some mocking song. You got to find something to scare them worse than the lightning did.

But what? Certainly not a lone boy on a horse. They'd trample him to pink gravy. What scared a spud? What could possibly be worse for a spud than being baked in a lightning bolt? It had to be something big, something terrible.

Brig tried to remember the stories his daddy had told him, stories handed down by spud wranglers since the earliest days. Many of the legends predated the arrival of the white man, and more often than not made no sense in the modern world. Stories about how the Quetzal flew the spirit of the potato northward from South America, or how an ancient tuber tribe went mad in the canyonlands of what was now Utah. Brig had never been interested in his father's stories, but now he wished he had paid more attention. There might have been a tidbit of wisdom in there that could help him now.

He could barely hear himself think over the roar of the stampede and the hoofbeats of Parley's horse, but he noticed with grim satisfaction that he was gaining on the herd. He could beat them to the canyon, but what could he do once he got there?

There was one thing that always scared a potato: the half-circle of arms over the head. No one knew why it struck such fear into the hearts of spuds, but its effect was undeniable. It was such a primal image to a spud that any kind of half-circle would make them skittish. Something as simple as an arched gateway could keep a ranch house's yard free of even the boldest spud.

Yes, the half-circle would scare a spud, but this herd was so vast that most of the spuds would never see him making the sign. He needed something bigger, and in the failing evening light, he needed something that would shine out like a beacon to the advancing herd.

There was only one chance. Joe Handy's construction crew. Brig had seen him working at the new Big Falls market just yesterday. He'd be working today. Brig glanced back at Hanged Man's Spike. If there were only more time!

He had managed to flank the herd. Coming down on to the plain, Brig knew what he had to do. The herd would follow the plain to hit Snake River Canyon about three miles from Big Falls City. He had to get to the City first, grab Joe Handy, then get there before them. There wasn't a second to waste.

His mouth set, Brig spurred towards Big Falls City.

———

"Man, you're plum loco!" Under the dust, Joe's face showed white as a sheet. Actually whiter than a spud wrangler's sheets. Standing on the bed of his ancient Ford pickup, Joe tightened the connections to a portable generator. "I'm on duty, and I ain't supposed to leave my place. And this," he pointed to the contents of the truck, "is supposed to run 24 hours a day."

"Yeah, well, get it running now," Brig snapped. In the west, Hanged Man's Spike speared the bottom of the sun.

"I ain't staying here. Them spuds'll push you right over the edge of the canyon."

The air shook with the rumble of the advancing spuds. A column of dust marked the herd. In maybe five minutes they'd be here. But the herd was tiring. That was good.

"You just get that equipment working. I'll be the one throwing the switch." Brig wiped his brow. Involuntarily, he glanced over the canyon edge. Four hundred feet straight down to a black rock floor. Far below he could see buzzards wheeling in the updraft. From here, they looked no bigger than gnats.

This had better work. If it didn't, mashed potato city, with Brig on the bottom. Bring on the gravy.

He looked back up just as the electrician's broad back disappeared over a lava outcropping to the east.

Damn! What a coward. For a second, Brig considered joining him. Then he jumped into the bed of the pickup and slapped Parley's horse on its rump. "Run for your life, boy." The horse bolted after the electrician. Brig hated to see it go, but if this didn't work and he went over the side of the canyon, the boss would resent losing a good horse.

Suddenly the spud herd burst into view. Not as tired as Brig had hoped. In front of them, frightened jackrabbits and a lone coyote scampered.

Brig pressed the start button on the generator motor. Damn. Nothing. The wall of spuds came nearer. Now Brig could smell the starch.

Forcing himself to stay calm, Brig tested each wire on the generator. Now the thundering spuds drowned all other sounds. Running at full speed, a jackrabbit thudded into the side of the pickup. It dropped to lie quivering in the dust.

A wire came loose in Brig's hand. Bad connection. He glanced up, and gasped. All he could see was a wall of spuds. His sweaty fingers shoved the wire into place, and he jabbed the starter button.

The generator motor whirred, coughed, and quit.

The reek of hot starch and potato peels clogged Brig's nostrils. The first few spuds splattered against the side of the pickup.

Brig jabbed the start button again.

The motor whirred, coughed, then roared into life. Quickly Brig flipped the light switch to "on."

From the very edge of Snake River Canyon, two gigantic golden arches lit up the Idaho sky. They were just yellow marquee lights on a wire frame, but they stood out stark and bold against the blackness beyond.

The oncoming herd recoiled. In a twisting, seething mass of brown, spuds bounded backwards, piling on top of the herds still streaming in from the plain. A mountain of spuds reared into the sky, looming over the low plain like some new volcanic cone. Then, gradually, the mass turned on itself, the herd streaming back north, northeast, northwest—any direction to escape those terrible glittering golden arches.

Exhausted, Brig stepped down off the pickup and lay down in the warm starch-smelling dust. He closed his eyes, wondering if spud wranglers would ever learn why the occult and archetypal symbol struck such fear into the hearts of spuds.

"Brig. Ya OK, son?"

Brig opened his eyes. Parley stood over him, bandages covering his chest. His arm lay in a sling.

"Parley. I thought you was dead."

"Not hardly, son."

"How are the..."

"The spuds? Well, I reckon they're about ten miles out in the desert by now, and a tireder and more docile pack of tubers you ain't never going to see in your life." Parley grinned. "Let the tenderfeet and the little boys round 'em up." He pulled a silver flask and an Idaho Spud candy bar from his saddle bag. "We wranglers got some serious resting to do."

GUERRILLA DEPREDATIONS—"YOUR MONEY OR YOUR LIFE!"—Sketched by W. D. Matthews.—[See Page 235.]

"You rustled my spuds. I can smell baker on your breath."

A FEW MINUTES IN THE PLANTATION BAR AND GRILL OUTSIDE WOODVILLE, MISSISSIPPI

STEVE PERRY

The New York Times *bestselling writer Steve Perry takes on an old idea in this original story and gives it a nifty* Pulphouse *twist. And his knowledge of the music in this story you can trust because he's been there.*

Steve wrote for Batman: The Animated Series, *did the novelization for* Star Wars: Shadows of the Empire, *and wrote numbers of books with Tom Clancy on the Net Force Series.*

Steve calls stories like this Wild Hair stories. I have loved every one of them I have had the pleasure to read. I think you will as well.

———

I was cleaning up when I heard a deep male voice behind me: "You know, in some places, they call what you do the Devil's music."

I was wiping the fretboard of my acoustic guitar with a rag dampened with a bit of fragrant lemon oil—the rosewood tends to want to dry out under the lights, and that's where we spend most of our time. Bright. Hot. Made worse, in the local weather. Still eighty-five degrees out there. The lemon oil fought the scent of stale beer, but it was no contest.

"Heard that one a time or two."

The wee hours shambled and slouched toward dawn. Except for us, a tired and cranky waitress clearing and clattering bottles, and a bartender restocking the beer cooler, the place was empty.

Just another gig. In a long line of gigs more or less like it.

Been a pretty good one, though. Nobody threw anything at me, only a couple of fights all evening. They came to listen.

After almost sixty years playing, I'd heard all the stories about what the blues were and what they meant. I believe that devil one probably came from a church-going woman frightened of what she heard when she caught her man playing blues instead of the gospel he was supposed to be practicing.

A long way from "What a Friend We Have in Jesus," to "Cocaine."

Or, maybe, it was just the Devil trying to claim the music for his own.

Wasn't his, the blues. They were humanity's music. A gift to help us get by.

I finished the fretboard, turned the guitar over and looked at the back. It was an unusual wood the luthier had used for the body, something called white ebony. It wasn't really white, more cream-colored, with wide streaks of black in it. The back and sides were made from that, the top from redwood. Instrument had a deep, mellow sound, made by an old hippie who lived on the Big Island of Hawaii.

I wore my belt with the front slid partway around my waist, to keep the guitar from developing belt-buckle rash. It gets scratched plenty anyway. You don't haul your instrument to hundreds of gigs without it picking up a few dings and dents. Banged into a mike stand there; a beer bottle knocked over some-where else. Had a woman puke on it once, though that was only because I was between her and the toilets.

I'd owned a lot worse axes over the years, maybe a couple that were as good. Action was high enough to play slide, and the pick-up worked well enough. If I couldn't reach an audience, it wasn't the guitar's fault.

Long way from where it was born, this guitar, out here in the backwoods of Mississippi.

I put the instrument into its case, closed the lid, latched the latches. Looked more closely at the guy.

He smiled.

Hard to guess his age. Could have been forty, from his general appearance, but he seemed older. He was tall, sharp-featured-hawk's nose, heavy eyebrows, thin lips revealing perfect teeth, with dark hair piled into a pompadour and slicked back with something that made it shine. Had a vaguely Middle Eastern look to him, weak-tea-colored skin.

He wore an expensive, gray summer suit, a darker, charcoal tie with a ruby stickpin, a pearl-colored shirt. Cowboy boots that matched the tie. Had a gold pinkie ring with a ruby that matched the tie-tack, only bigger.

Way overdressed for a honky-tonk like this one.

I hadn't seen him come in, and clothed like that among the shitkickers and rednecks? I would have thought I couldn't have missed him, but it had been crowded most of the set. Seventy-five, eighty people packed into a room designed for fifty, bottled beer flowing, lubricating the crowd as they listened. I had them, most of them, enthralled, and they had me, because no matter how good you are, you need listeners as much as they need players.

And, sometimes, I get lost, so deep into the music, I don't pay attention to the world around me. Fine feeling, that, but with some drawbacks. Was in a place that caught on fire once, and if somebody running for the exit hadn't kicked the plug to my amp out? I might have cooked there before I noticed.

"You're very good," he said.

"Thank you, I appreciate that."

I bent and coiled my amp cord. The little amp I use isn't much, not enough for a big room full of people, but it works okay as a monitor piggybacked onto the house PA, and even a rat hole like The Plantation Bar and Grill outside Woodville here had its own sound system.

I tucked the cord into the amp's case, zipped the top shut. All packed and ready to roll.

Live music still pulled them in, out in the country on a hot August night.

"You should be playing better venues," he said.

"You an agent?"

"Among other things."

I shrugged. "I'm doing okay on my own."

Of a moment, his eyes sparkled with an inner light. "I have contacts. I can put you into stadiums, I can put you into arenas. There's always room for a man of your talent and skill. You could be famous. Rich. Have your pick of women. A second act, a comeback."

"Never was there," I said. "What comeback?"

He chuckled. "Still and all. You could be like Son House. Etta James. Howlin' Wolf."

"I'm on the downside of seventy," I said. "That doesn't call to me like it did forty, even thirty years ago."

"You're not getting any younger, either. Things are going to happen. Your body will betray you. Money would make that easier."

"George Harrison left more than a hundred million behind," I said. "Tom Petty wasn't missing any meals. Elvis owned his own drugstore."

"They would have made it farther, they'd signed with me."

"You got that much juice?"

"After a fashion, yes. Nobody lives forever, but my clients hang around longer, that's part of our deal, I look after them. You could have twenty, thirty more years."

He glanced around, waved one hand. Had long, manicured nails. "You're better than this, way better. Don't you want people to hear you?"

"People hear me."

"Too few. It's a waste of your ability. You could move tens of thousands at a time. I can see it."

Money not enough? Young and complaint women willing to

take the time to help an old man get off? Best tables at the best restaurants? Not them, either?

Well, how about reaching a *big* audience? There was the giant ice cream cone in the sky. A huge audience, rapt, moved. The energy of thirty or forty thousand people, all focused on your every word, every lick, with you, and feeding that love back to you...?

Hard to turn away from that temptation, hey?

I smiled. "I was doing some session work in New York, back in the late sixties, early seventies. Playing a Telecaster. Clapton came into the studio, to sit in on somebody's record. He was always a bluesman, even after he turned into a rock star. When the session was done, he offered me a job. I could have played with him and Duane Allman, could have gone down to Miami, to record 'Layla.'"

He said, "Allman liked Gibsons, Clapton was a Stratocaster man—that's how you can tell them apart on the record, the differences in tone. Would have been something with a Tele in the mix. I can almost hear it."

Yeah. I had thought about that a time or ten.

"You know the story about the piano solo? Jim Gordon, the drummer, was sneaking back into the studio at night to record his own material, and they caught him playing that. Made him a deal —he could keep swiping the studio time, if they could use that piece as the coda on the tune.

"He was schizophrenic, Gordon was. He killed his mother. Beat her head in with a claw hammer, stabbed her. Sixteen-to-life. Probably gonna die in Vacaville. Still thinks she is alive."

"Uh huh."

"Duane swiped his main riff on that song from Albert King. Sped up some, but that's what it was."

"I heard that."

"But you passed on a chance to record what would become

one of the classic blues-rock tracks of all time with two of the best guitarists in the world."

"I did."

"Why?"

"Couple things. They liked coke and heroin in those days. Not a path I wanted to go down."

"On the fast road to hell, you figured? Burn brighter, but half as long?"

I nodded. "Eric cleaned up eventually, got off it. Duane killed himself riding his Harley a year and some later. And you know about Jim. But that's not really it. They had it, they loved it, the blues, they were better than good, but they moved into rock. Nothing wrong with that, but..." I let it trail off.

The man in grey nodded. "So it's about purity."

"Three chords and the truth. Well, that, and a turnaround."

He smiled at me, flashing those perfect teeth again. "You have more than that."

"But that part is enough."

"You don't have to change. There is a place for it."

I shook my head.

"Got to be something I can offer you."

I pretended to think about it.

I was about to speak when Sara arrived.

Sara doesn't just walk into place, she *sweeps* in. It almost as if somebody is playing tabla, sarangi, and flute soundlessly behind her. Can't quite hear it, but you can feel it in the vibrations. Best of Bollywood, but no flash, just the sometimes-buried substance.

She's handsome—not beautiful, not in a classical way, but there is an unmistakable aura about her. It's certainly not her clothes—she was wearing faded jeans, a yellow T-shirt, and sandals, with her blue-black hair piled up and pinned into a kind of squirrel's nest that wasn't impressive, but somehow was part of a total look that always made most everybody stop and stare. She could have been any age, too. Young, old, timeless...

The tired waitress and the bartender quit what they were doing to watch her, and the guy trying to sign me didn't look, ah, but he *felt* her.

He shook his head. "Fuck me."

Then he did turn to look at her.

"Saraswati."

"Levi."

"Yours." Not a question.

"He is."

"No wonder he didn't jump on it" He shook his head. "Blues isn't that old. It's a local product."

"Music is music. Never yours, no matter how much you wish it."

She was human enough to a casual glance, but if you knew how, if you looked in just the right way, you could see the extra arms. Best sitar player there ever was, so it was said, and I didn't doubt it. I'd heard her play guitar, and nobody else could come within a thousand miles. Listening to her play could bring tears of joy to a stone statue.

Some say she is part of the Trinity, with Lakshmi and Parvati; others say she was born of the primal ocean, and that Brahma is her father, sort of. We never talked about it, so I don't know. One doesn't pry into a Goddess's business.

Levi—for "Leviathan"—sighed. He looked at me. "I can make you a better deal."

She laughed. "I am Music," she said. "You? You are Fallen, and you can't get back up. You have nothing with which to tempt him."

He shook his head again.

She said, "You ready?"

"Yep."

"Let me get the amp."

I nodded. I took my guitar, she picked up the amp in its case as if it weighed nothing, and we headed for the door.

I nodded at the Devil on our way out.

Just another gig...

GRAYMATTERS

DAVID STIER

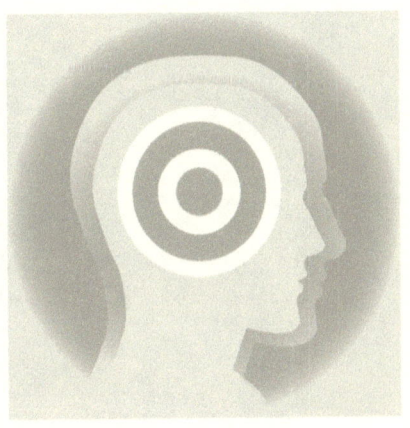

I have had the pleasure for a few years now of reading David Stier's powerful stories for Fiction River *and now for* Pulphouse Fiction Magazine. *To say that I am a major fan of David's work would be an understatement.*

David never shies away from the really tough topics, and makes the characters in his stories real and gritty, often fitting perfectly with the rough situations. This original story is no exception and will make you a fan of David Stier as well.

———

Colin Murphy crossed Front Street toward his girlfriend, Julie's, condo. A welcome gust of ocean breeze cleared out some of last night's poker win celebration. On the offshore rocks of Cowell beach, seals *arfed* loudly, at themselves and anyone who cared to listen.

Not too bad a head, considering all the blackjack and beer.

As Colin neared Julie's condo complex, the hair on the back of his neck rose. His eyeballs started to itch.

Dude, not now.

Bo Jangles, back again. Ol' Bo never brought warm and fuzzy feelings. The day Colin's mom had died—run over by a drunk driver—his brain had been squeezed in a full court press. Damned migraines could last for days—especially when he used the *talent*. Ol' Bo really made him pay, from a tap, tap, tapping on the back of his eyes to a wicked stomp and grind, depending on the mental chops he used.

Just peachy. Larry, Julie's condo manager, stood out front watering the lawn. Colin slowed, preparing for the usual smiley face act. Dude gave him a serious case of the creeps. Filmy fish eyes, crooked schnoz, and limp, flabby lips. Put that combo with a spindly fifties potbelly, and you had one of the ugliest mofos this side of a Stephen King novel.

But hey, the good looks door had slammed in Colin's face too, so that wasn't the prob. Besides, his *talent* had proved that the prettiest angel face or handsomest lantern-jawed kisser could cloak the biggest nasty around. What he hated was how Larry drooled over Julie. And the one time Colin had looked inside the perv's head had confirmed his bad vibes to the max.

As he turned into the complex, Larry looked up. Huh? No oily smile for one, and a mean payback glare for another. Those filmy eyes seemed ready to pop out of the old fart's head.

Better have a look-see.

"Hey Larry, my man." He sidestepped the stream of water when Larry turned. "How's it hangin?"

Colin slapped the old dude on the shoulder, then let his hand slide to his throat, found the carotid artery's rapid pulse.

Too late, Larry tried to back away. Colin held fast, made eye contact. Larry's peepers opened wide enough for Colin to make out a stereo view of his own reflected features.

Colin concentrated on Larry's pulse, which crept slowly up his arm. He focused on the dilated pupils, feeling for the presence of the optic nerves, then let his mind follow the twin trails into the pathways of Larry's brain.

Images flashed by: *Julie's window; Julie and two of her buds laughing and playing an online computer game; Julie's rent statement on Larry's comp screen, "Rent Past Due" noted in red font; a fantasy image of Larry at Julie's door, showing her the printout; Julie stepping aside; Larry moving past; the door closing; then real-world rage when the door slams in his face.*

Colin quelled the urge to give Larry's brain a squeeze. This play would cost him enough. Already he felt the beginnings of a migraine. He called up the image of the computer's ledger, erased the rent past due knowledge from Larry's brain, then planted the thought that Julie had paid her rent through March. As a bonus he inserted the feeling that it was ol' Larry-Boy's lucky day. The blackjack table at the Ocean Card Lounge beckoned. Colin backed out of the slime's head, stepped back and waited.

Larry staggered, lost the garden hose. The water stream cascaded down the sidewalk and into the gutter, a fitting metaphor indeed.

"Whoa," Colin said. "Sorry, man. Guess I tripped." Larry's eyes gained a little focus. "You'd think they'd fix the friggin' sidewalks around here, huh?" Colin stooped, picked up the hose, handed it to Larry who'd snapped out of the trance.

A sudden smile transformed Larry's face. "Sure thing, Colin," he said. "Great day, ain't it?"

"Damn straight, dude. Say…" Colin reached for his wallet. "I got Julie's rent here."

Larry moved quickly to the spigot, turned off the water, coiled the hose and hung it on the rack. "She paid two months' rent last night. Good thing too, since she was a month late."

Colin nodded. "Good for her, huh? What's the rush?"

The smile morphed into a crescent-moon leer.

"Today's my lucky day. Don't know why, but I'm gonna do something about it."

Colin nodded, slapped Larry on the back. "Gotta go with those vibes when you get 'em," he said.

"Effin' A," said Larry. "Later."

———

"Hey, babe," Colin said, as he and Julie embraced then kissed. "Think I see a New Year's resolution or three. What's up?"

For something sure as hell *was* up. She'd spit shined the living room of her condo. Even cleaned the screens of her computer and TV, and the glass top of the scuffed coffee table. If she and her buds had been playing *Dragon Age* last night, she must've worked all morning scouring and scrubbing up.

Back in the day he'd learned the hard way to stay out of his girlfriend's mind. More than one relationship had crashed and burned until he'd learned that tune.

With a light caress to his face, Julie pushed away, headed toward the kitchen.

"Looks like you could use a coffee or three," she said. "Must have had a wild night. Don't have any new competition to worry about, do I?"

Colin shrugged, smiled, and winked. Then he sat down on the couch. The place smelled like she'd spent about a hundred bucks on room deodorizer too. The stuck-up feline presence of Kashi, her pet Persian, was nowhere to be had.

Julie set down a cup of coffee on the table, took her own cup and curled into the beanbag chair across the tiny room. The aroma of quality dark roast erased the strawberry deodorizer scent.

She'd dyed her hair last night too; purple, and it looked good. Hell, she'd look good with a shaved head—had, in fact. A new eyebrow ring too. The migraine had him by the short hairs so he nixed the urge to find out if the beanbag was big enough for two.

"Hair looks great, babe. You must've been busy all night. Thought you and your band of happy warriors were going after *Corypheus*?"

Her smile faded. She looked half a heartbeat from a sob fest. Not possible that Larry's little game could send her into crash-and-burn mode. He'd seen her ice hardcore bikers with a single bored glance. Even threatening her with eviction shouldn't have laid her this low.

"Where's the cat?" he asked.

Outside, Larry's old Detroit beater backfired as it sputtered to life. Julie's eyes hardened and her mouth turned down on one side, proof that a certain condo manager had better watch out.

Best of luck, Larry-Boy. May you draw to dead hands all day.

She took a sip of coffee. He did the same, waiting her out.

"Can you loan me some money?" she said. "Larry's been bugging me about the rent."

"Yeah." Colin slouched back on the couch. "The old fart hit me up on the way in. Said you were a month behind too." He waved her anxiety away. "All taken care of, babe. I got lucky at The Lounge last night. You're paid through March."

The doorbell chimed. An annoyed look appeared and quickly faded from Julie's face. Since it was her pad, she got the honors. Sine waves on the walls and renewed itching behind his eyes signaled another Bo Jangles appearance so he moved to a position behind the opening door.

"Oh," Julie said. "Hi Doug."

Colin eased past Julie. Dude looked upscale for The Cruz—even this overpriced dump. Hair a little too well-groomed, clothes a little too designer for Colin's taste.

"Excuse me, Julie." Out-Of-Place said. "I was wondering if—"

She followed the dude's eyes, met Colin's questioning look, gave that relieved smile that told Colin all he needed to know about this little scene.

"Doug, meet Colin. My boyfriend."

Colin met the guy's open gaze. "How's it going, dude?" he said, then stuck out his hand, making a cursory search upon contact just to be safe.

Seemed okay. Just thinking about used books, CDs, and grabbing a smoke.

"Quite well, Colin, thank you. I'm in the process of moving to Santa Cruz—directly downstairs, in fact—but don't yet have the key. That was supposed to be supplied this morning, but said individual is nowhere to be found."

Definitely weird. "That sounds like Larry. Guy fades in and out like a busted neon sign."

"Well, that's the problem. I've got some boxes here but nowhere to put them." Doug looked over to Julie. "Any possibility of leaving them here till I bring over the next load? Should only be a few hours."

Longer than that, man, unless ol' Larry hits a real bad streak of luck, heh, heh.

"Sure, Doug," Julie said. "We'll be here all day." She pointed to an open corner of the living room. "Just dump them over there."

"Hey, man, I'll give you a hand." And together Colin and Doug schlepped the stuff upstairs. Before the final load, Doug pulled out a pack of coffin nails. "Mind if I smoke?"

Colin stepped back a couple steps. "Dude, actually I do. I grew up with tobacco smoke twenty-four-seven. I avoid it now like the plague. Sorry."

After Doug had asked for directions to Logos, the local used book and CD store, they'd parted the old ways, so to speak. Good thing, too. Dude loved to smoke—or so it smelled. Colin hated tobacco. His ma had smoked like a chimney. Her lung-fried cough was a sound he'd take to the grave. If that drunk driver hadn't got her, she'd probably have kacked in another year from the smokes.

As soon as the door closed, Julie's smile faded.

"Thanks for paying the rent. I'll pay it back when I get paid for that game design—hopefully next week."

"No prob, babe. We're a team. You'd do it for me—have done, in fact, so forget it. But that ain't all, is it?"

Julie glanced to the closed bedroom door.

He sipped a fresh cup of coffee, using it to hide the scowl. *Bingo,* or rather, *Kashi.* "The cat again, right? What's wrong with it this time?"

Her back stiffened. She set the cup down on the coffee table. Coffee slopped from the cup and spread in an expanding brown pool across the glass.

"Didn't you just clean that?" He went to the kitchen for a rag, and wiped up the spill.

"*The cat* has a name, you know," she said after he'd sat back down.

He gulped the brew, a big mistake, because now his tongue would have that raspy burned feeling for the rest of the morning.

"Okay, already. What's wrong with Kashi, *this time*? That feline snob don't like me, so why should I like it?" Before she could respond, he raised his hand in surrender. "Look, I know Persians only bond to the owner, that's cool, I get it and I ain't crushed about it, but every time I step into your pad, his little pug nose shoots up to the sky and he looks at me like something that got stuck on one of his furry paws."

Her lower lip trembled. She brushed at her eyes. "The vet says he has feline leukemia." Then the tears came and he was across the room and holding her in his arms.

———

"Okay, gents, ante up," the dealer said as he shuffled the cards for another round of Texas Hold 'Em.

Christ, amazing how a deck of cards could morph anyone into a cheesy Bret Maverick imitation and the Ocean Card Lounge into the Long Branch Saloon.

Colin glanced over at the blackjack table. Larry was hard at it, and from the sour look on his face, he was in epic fail mode. He glanced over and Colin waved. Larry scowled and returned to his game of twenty-two.

After Maverick, Colin anted up ten bucks. The other three

clowns—two maniacs and a newbie—did the same. Maverick dealt hole cards all around and then the flop.

Seven of clubs and duce of diamonds. A seven-duce again?

He'd expected to win enough for the kitty chemo by now. He checked his watch. Damn.

"Yo, dude. What's the prob?" Maniac Numero Uno, to the left of Maverick, said as he threw down a Jackson. "Another crap hand?"

Colin looked up from his cards, made eye contact with the acne-scarred face.

Numero Uno's grin widened, exposing a set of tobacco-stained teeth circled by a pair of thin lips under squinty eyes and a droopy mustache. The dweeb picked up the smoldering cigarette and took a drag, careful to blow the smoke away from Colin. By law, smoking was illegal, but the owners and players ignored that little statute. Colin loved playing poker enough to put up with the smoky stench and watery eyes.

Numero Uno had lost two Benjamins so far. The other maniac gambler had lost more. One decent flop and he could clean these chumps out in a single hand. But today, good flops were like bad Reno lays. Expensive and loaded with clap.

Colin stuck around till fifth street, then folded.

Now it was Colin's deal, and he hoped his luck would change.

"Bet you can't even deal yourself a monster," Numero Uno said after Colin dealt everyone's hole cards, burned a card, then dealt the flop, a bullet and two kings.

He kept his poker face in place as he scoped out the two aces he held.

A full boat already. Hot diggity damn. About friggin' time.

The other maniac—Jesse—threw down a Jackson. "Ha, ha, you chumps! This time you're all goin' down."

"Like hell, dudeski," said Numero Uno, who called and raised another Jackson.

Colin, Newbie, and Maverick called.

Jesse's cheeks reddened and his eyes got very large.

Four kings, maybe? Probably two pair.

"You're all bluffing," Jesse said, and threw down two more Jacksons.

With a face like that, dude shouldn't play high stakes. Colin would do his best to learn him that fact.

"The hell you say," Numero Uno said, then called and raised another two Jackson's.

"Ha, ha!" said Maverick. "Bout friggin' time we had a real man's hand." He called and raised a Benjamin, then glanced at Colin and Newbie.

"That's it for me," Newbie said. "Too rich for my blood."

"When you grow a pair, come on back." Numero Uno said.

Newbie slowly stood, shook his head. Colin nodded. Newbie nodded back, then he tuned and left.

Dude had class. Had only lost a Grant. He knew when to fold, too.

Colin checked out the remaining three clowns. Identical we're-super-duper-and-you're-nothing-but-a-loser looks were plastered across their faces. It would be sweet taking these idiots down a peg or twenty. They'd gone tiltski so it should be easy-fucking-peasy to sandbag them all. He called but didn't raise—let the coffehousing chumps think he was drawing to a dead hand.

He dealt fourth street. An off-suit queen. Bets progressed. The pot grew by a few Cs. Everyone stayed in.

Fifth street was the last bullet.

Nut city.

Maverick threw in three Jacksons. Numero Uno called. Jesse raised another Benjamin, and before Colin could bet, Numero Uno called and raised another Benjamin.

Colin leaned back, allowing a shit-eating grin to form.

"My, my," Colin said as he threw in three Benjamins and a

Jackson to call, then took out four Grants and threw them in as well. "Let's see who's got a pair now."

The three high rollers studied their cards. Colin kept the smile in place, checking each face in turn.

With a maybe-I-screwed-the-pooch scowl, Numero Uno dug into his hip pocket, peeled off four Grants, and threw them into the pot.

"I think you're bluffing, chump."

Colin shrugged, rubbed his mouth with the back of his hand, and faked a look of disappointment. Jesse took the bait and called too. After another long pause, Maverick did the same.

"Okay, dickwad," Numero Uno said. "Let's see the cards."

"You gents know anything about World War Two?" Colin asked.

Their puzzled looks would be an image he'd remember for beaucoup days to come.

"It's like this, see: there was this American general that had the best one-word reply to a Nazi ultimatum. And that, my friends, is a poifect fitski for this here hand." Colin threw down his two bullets.

"Nuts."

The three losers stared at each other in drop-jawed shock as Colin raked in the humongous pile of dead presidents.

"It's been a pleasure, boys. Till the next time."

Two minutes later he was out the door with over $3K in his pocket.

———

Before Colin had gone five blocks, someone grabbed his shoulder from behind and spun him around.

Big surprise. Numero Uno and Jesse, looking more than a little pissed off.

"Okay, dipstick," Numero Uno said, "this can be painless or not. Hand over the bread."

The good news: Jesse wasn't wearing sunglasses. The bad news: Numero Uno was. Too bad, considering that Jesse had a pale face to go along with a scared shitless look.

"Where's Maverick?" Colin asked.

"Maverick? Who the hell's—" Jesse said after he wiped his mouth with the back of a shaking hand.

Numero Uno moved closer and grabbed Colin by the lapels of his leather coat. "No balls to take back what's his. *That's* where he is." Numero Uno smiled, his thin lips emphasizing the messed-up teeth. "But we'll find a use for it, huh, Jess?"

From the look on Jesse's face, what he could really use was some Pepto or TP, cause he looked ready to puke or crap his pants.

Numero Uno shook Colin again. "Cough it up."

Breath smelled bad enough to gag a maggot. God, Colin hated smoker's breath.

"Oh, please, Mister," Colin said, trying to get the turn-to-jelly whine just right. "Don't hurt me."

"Okay, punk—"

Colin smashed the heel of his right boot into the chump's toes. The loser let go and got out half a scream before Colin's right fist clocked his left jaw. Numero Uno hit the deck. The back of his head smacked the asphalt with a meaty *fwop*. Colin shook his hand to lessen the pain.

Jesse froze, not knowing whether to shit or hang up. Colin moved in, grabbed him by the neck, and made eye contact.

"Make like an ice cube and freeze," he said. Then he probed the guy's mind.

He'd blown his rent money?

"Well, bud, life *is* unfair, ain't it?" Colin felt for the cash in his hip pocket, pulled out $200. "You hear me?"

37

"Yeah, I hear you," Jesse mumbled while staring past Colin's shoulder.

"That's good, man. Now listen close." He stuffed the money in Jesse's shirt pocket. "You ought to bag poker. You blow at it."

Colin probed a little deeper. Images flashed by: *A rice paddy; two GI's, one dragging the other who'd lost both legs above the knee; red signal smoke swirling; a helicopter landing; about twenty black-pajama-clad Asian types racing to prevent the rescue; Jesse, the unwounded GI, standing, firing a grenade launcher; several Vietcong being blown to hell; Jesse firing his M-16 until all the VC were down; one of the helicopter's crew dragging Jesse toward the chopper; another two carrying Mr. Peg-leg-in-training—*

The fog returned. Colin followed the billowing mist.

Next: *Jesse, now a civilian and drunk as the proverbial skunk, being cuffed; flashing red and blue lights; two wrecked cars; an ambulance pulling away; then Jesse in a jail cell, spread-eagled by two muscle-bound, tatted-out goons; a third even bigger goon sporting even more tats, most of the state slammer variety, laughing as he ripped Jesse's pants down—*

Colin yanked himself back to the alley. Jesse stood before him, pupils still dilated, a line of drool tracing a wet trail down his face. Colin stepped back. Jesse blinked.

What now? He could maybe do him a favor and erase the rape, but somehow that didn't feel right. Colin and morality were at best very distant cousins, but he drew the line at that kind of theft. He looked up and down the alley—still clear—and made eye contact again.

"Look, man, snap the fuck out of it. So what? You wasted a bunch of guys who were trying to waste you, a buddy lost his legs but you saved his ass, then you ended up getting fudge packed. For Chrissake, dude, remember the man you were in Viet Nam. You gonna be a loser all your life? You *suck* at poker too and I think it would be smartski to quit." He stuffed another $500 in Jesse's shirt pocket, then snapped the link.

"Give your landlord a sob story about the rest of the rent. Tell him you got mugged. This should help with that." Colin stepped back and punched Jesse in the eye. The dude's back hit the wall and he slid down to a sitting position.

"Hope you stay awake for a week, wondering about those seven C's."

Colin straightened his jacket, bent down to make sure Numero Uno was still breathing, then rifled his pockets, found the cigarettes and butane lighter, slipped them inside his inner coat pocket. Let him buy another pack if he had any bread left. Coffin nails were the first thing losers like that went for whenever life kicked their ass.

————

"Here you go, sweetnic." He fanned twenty-five Benjamins and waved them back and forth. Julie's eyes opened so wide that he thought they'd pop out of her head.

She ran across the room, grabbed him around the neck, and landed a big wet one mostly on the mouth.

He returned the kiss. His arms went around her back, and their bodies melded together. She smelled of strawberries and vanilla. His tongue traced the outline of her front teeth.

She broke away, face red and breathing ragged. "This isn't a good time, Colin. I've got to get Kashi to the vet."

Colin took a step in her direction. His hand shot to her throat and squeezed. Julie's eyes widened even more, but this time in fear.

Not a good time? Hadn't he earned a reward for saving that miserable cat's frigging hide? Maybe what she needed was a good bitch slap or three. He pushed her away, took out Numero Uno's pack of smokes and started to light up.

Julie massaged her throat, looking at Colin as though he'd grown a second head.

"When did you start smoking?"

He looked at the unlit cigarette, broke it in half and stuffed it in a pocket. Had he just tried to strangle his girlfriend?

"Sorry," he said. "Don't know what got into me. That shouldn't have happened."

He set the bills on the table, tried to smile, but it felt as stiff as Mr. Happy had been just seconds before.

"Colin, what's—"

"I'm sorry, I—" He opened the door. "Good luck at the vet's," he said, and stumbled outside and down the stairs.

———

What the hell was he doing?

Across the street in Julie's condo, two shadows passed the front room window. Colin's gut knotted up in something that would have done Mr. Gordian proud.

Who was in there with her? Her door opened. Doug, outlined in the light from the living room, carrying one of his boxes downstairs and returning for another. Colin watched for a couple of trips. Doug turned and looked in his direction. Their eyes met and Doug smiled.

The hair on Colin's neck tingled and his eyes throbbed in brief pain. No way could he be recognized. The street was too dark and he stood in the shadows.

He checked his watch: nine p.m.

He pulled out the cigarettes, looked at them for a minute, then took one and lit up. After a couple of drags he threw it down and ground it under his heel.

Julie's living room lights went out. Doug walked downstairs with the last box and closed his door. Colin crossed the street. At Julie's front door, he turned and headed downtown. What he needed were lights and other people. Yeah, a beer or ten at the Catalyst should make it right.

———

The Catalyst had been a bad idea: too many lights, too many people, and way too much noise. After a quick beer, Colin left and wandered Pacific Avenue until the lights and people there got to him as well.

Now he stood in a dank backstreet behind Pacific Avenue. The three back doors, lit by pale orange sodium fixtures, jaundiced the walls and wet cobbles in a sickly pale glow. An offshore breeze kicked in and the ocean air blew down the 1920s-era alley. In the distance, the pounding Pacific Ocean waves beat an uneven cadence. Maybe a walk on the beach was what he needed.

He wondered what had happened to Jesse and Numero Uno. For reasons he couldn't scope, the thought of changing places with either dude seemed very appealing right now. He held his right hand up to the light. Had it really wrapped itself around Julie's neck?

"Thanks for the directions, man. I got some good deals."

Colin spun around. The smiling face he could just make out in the dark looked familiar. Doug? He tried to remember the last time someone had surprised him like that and came up empty, like the feeling in his heart.

"Dude, didn't your mama ever tell you it ain't smart to sneak up on someone at night?"

Doug's smile widened. Colin tried to make out the eyes, but

all he could see were two black pits below a Navy watch cap. Doug also wore a dark trench coat.

Doug pulled out a cigarette and lit up. The light gave Colin a quick glimpse of the eyes, and what he saw sent a chill down his spine. Twin tombstones didn't even begin to describe them. It was more like twin mass graves from places like Kosovo or Rwanda. Why'd he miss that this morning?

"Smoke?" Doug asked.

Colin reached for the pack, then drew his hand back. He hated tobacco. His ma's cough echoed inside his head. A nagging voice echoed there as well.

Why does lighting up feel so right?

"I've been following you for a while, man," Doug said. "And dude, I do think we both have something in common. Something we both want too."

Mr. Out-of-Place—or better yet, Without-a-Trace, if what he'd just said was true, and the sick feeling in Colin's gut told him that it was—shivered and placed his hands inside his trench coat pockets.

"What, you eat organic?" Colin said. "Great, but old CDs don't exactly float my boat."

"That's good, Colin. The first one in particular, but those two observations weren't what I had *in mind*. Get it?" He smiled, and the dark alley and orange lighting made it seem more like a leer. "Besides, I never mentioned CDs."

"Well," Colin said, wishing the Buck Knife he'd left at home was sheathed on his belt instead, "if its beer, you must know I only had one."

A look of annoyance crossed Doug's face. He shook his head. "No, I'm talking about—how best to put it?—ah, yes: *Graymatters*. I've never met someone with similar talents, my friend. When you tried reading me this morning, I was surprised and almost let you through, but managed to plant a liking for tobacco in your sneaky little mind instead. Seems it took, huh? I wonder, did anything else?"

The image of his hand wrapped around Julie's throat flashed behind Colin's eyes.

Doug grinned, his shoulders tensed. Now he grasped something long and metallic in his right hand.

"Damn if your taste in women didn't trip over to me, too."

Colin swung, aiming for the jaw. Doug dodged, and the blow hit the side of his head, sending the watch cap flying into the shadows.

A searing pain lanced Colin's side. Doug moved away. Colin felt something warm and wet run down his stomach and leg. Looked like Buck Knives were something else they had in common, but odds were *this* one had seen long and frequent use. He pressed his hand to his side, and leaned against the wall. Let him think he'd hit a homerun. Maybe he had, but then again, maybe not.

Doug relaxed his stance. "Sorry, man, but in our little community, two's a crowd. I'll give Julie your love." Then he lunged.

Colin dropped to one knee, and clamped his bloody hand around Doug's knife-hand wrist. A back door light illuminated Doug's face. A line of sweat ran down Doug's forehead and along the bridge of his nose. It reached the tip, hung there for a moment, then fell to earth. Colin imagined it splashing on the cobbles, maybe a prequel to something colored red.

His leg almost buckled, but he managed to stand and force Doug's hand up and over his head. They stood face-to-face.

"Ever wonder how it feels when a mind dies, Colin? Stealing lives beats sex every time."

Besides stale tobacco, Doug's breath smelled like a soulless kind of hunger. Colin's leg again started to buckle. Doug's eyes locked with his. A coldness crept into the edges of Colin's mind.

The knife hand descended, bloody point two inches from Colin's left eye.

"The eyes are the windows of the soul, right?" Doug's smile reappeared. "But in your case they're the road to hell."

Another hand covered Colin's in a crushing grip, and the knife moved away from his eye. A look of surprise, anger, then terror crossed Doug's face. The knife moved up, over, then down into Doug's gut with a wet ripping sound.

Doug grunted and collapsed, then Colin passed out, a suffocating smell of blood the last thing he remembered.

———

Colin woke to the feeling of painful pressure on his side. He opened his eyes. Jesse's face, one eye swollen half-shut, mouth slanted to the side, giving an impression of faint anger and contempt.

He took Colin's left hand, roughly placed it over the knife wound. "Press here," he said. "Looks like he missed a vital organ, but you could still bleed out."

The scared-shitless look Colin remembered from this afternoon had been replaced with the piercing stare of a former combat vet. The smell of fear and brittle shame was gone from Jesse, too.

Jesse stood. "Been looking for *you* all day, dudeski. Guess I really do blow at poker. I can't remember why I started to play that shitty game but for some reason I think you deserve credit for teaching me that lesson."

Jesse stooped, and rifled Colin's pockets till he came up with the cell phone, dialed 911, and dropped the phone in Colin's lap. Then he stuffed something into Colin's shirt pocket.

"Thanks but no thanks, chump. You earned them fair and square."

Colin looked down at the street, away from Jesse's contempt.

He waited till the footsteps faded, then picked up the cell.

Colin gave the location, then hug up. Doug's body lay a few feet away. He felt in his pocket, pulled out the seven crumpled Benjamins and Numero Uno's pack of smokes. In the distance, the sound of a siren grew closer.

He threw the bills and butts down the alley as far as he could.

THE CLOCKWORK MAN'S CANTEEN

J. STEVEN YORK

This original story by J. Steven York is one of the best pure Western stories I have ever read, even though the hero of the story is a wind-up man. It's seamless and masterful and has a ton of heart.

And that is what makes it a perfect Pulphouse *story. I am honored to have it in this issue.*

Wow, would this make a great television series. You'll see what I mean when you get finished reading the story.

Steve is also doing a really fun and off-the-wall internet comic series, one of which he has allowed me to put in each issue of Pulphouse *on the back page. Don't miss those either.*

———

Though I am a clockwork man and have no need for water, I have learned from painful experience to always take a full canteen with me when I ride into the desert. I have learned that even a wind-up man made of brass and iron can thirst, and that want of water can kill us near sure as any man of flesh and bone.

My lesson in the matter began a handful of years after the Civil War, as my wonderful clockwork horse Piston and I rode west out of the little Nevada town of Las Vegas.

We were very far from my dark days as an artilleryman in the Army of the Confederacy on the bloody battlefield at Gettysburg, and my more recent troubles in Texas. With each day we moved into the vast emptiness of the far west, my normally taciturn spirits lifted. I had come to love the vast, open spaces, stark terrain, and lack of people, both flesh and metal, to involve me in their troubles.

Though many misfortunes I had come to believe that companionship led me only to trouble and grief, and that in these empty spaces I might finally find the peace I craved.

Though I knew the place ahead had been named Death Valley by the Forty-Niners who decades before had come to California in search of gold and silver, we rode into it with little fear or concern. It had been my understanding that thirst and heat were the killers of men in this place, and as I have said, we had no need of water, Piston and I, and we do not feel or suffer from any heat much less greater than it takes to melt our metal hides.

To me, Death Valley was just a place of solitude and beauty.

But I was to learn that my understanding of the frailties of men was sorely limited, and that the place held mortal dangers for creatures of metal as well.

The only immediate need Piston and I had as we began our journey into this most severe of wildernesses was our need of winding, and by this point in my journey even that was less of a concern that it once had been.

Piston had come to me out of the chaos of battle, without instruction or much more knowledge of his nature than his name. His origins were unknown to me, and if there was another quite like him, I had never heard of it.

It took me years to unravel some of his secrets, and one of these was that he was a winder-mill unto himself. Not only was his mainspring equipped with a take-off fitting to wind other clockwork men such as myself, but through ingenious attachments—hidden in a compartment under his saddle, or improvised using common materials such as rope and tree branches—his spring could be wound using animal power, water, or wind.

Finding suitable wind, not too soft and not too harsh, at the top of a rocky ridge, I camped and set up the little windmill hidden under the saddle. It took several days, but presently both our military-grade mainsprings were wound to capacity. There was little doubt we could make it to the mining town of Darwin, which I had been told waited beyond the far edge of the great Valley. If I was wrong about that, I knew we had only to hunker down to conserve our springs, and wait the return of favorable wind.

And so it was without care that we journeyed into the valley called Death. We left our encampment on the bluff at dawn, and with no hurry. We had no map, only some general directions and descriptions of landmarks given me by an old miner back in Las Vegas, and the magnetic compass built into my artilleryman's brain.

In that initial euphoria, I found Death Valley to be a wondrous place. Devoid as it mostly was of soil or vegetation, it seemed as though the skin of the world had been pulled back and its inner working laid bare.

Hills and mountains surrounded the place, jagged and tortured as though freshly pushed out of the ground. Stone came in all colors and types, often marking the cliffs and mountain-sides in bold stripes or crazy-quilts of mixed colors. In the depths of the valley floor, one could see the blindingly white lakes of salt toward which Piston and I descended.

I had been across desert and plains before, and so I had seen big skies, but somehow there, with the flat and barren expanse of the valley floor, the surrounding mountain peaks, and majestic clouds that cast dark shadows below them in lieu of rain, the sky seemed even bigger.

I was especially delighted with the heat, for as I have said, I could not feel it. But in this place, especially, I could see it. It shimmed and twisted the air, distorting light itself to create wondrous illusions, of lakes that moved away or evaporated as one approached, and of hilltops that seemed to hover in the sky.

Finally we came down to the salt itself, and found the surface cracked into scales, as though we moved across the hide of some great, albino serpent. Ahead of us the air shimmered like mercury, and the bases of the mountains beyond were hidden in a lake of mirages. We rode on, and something dark seemed to take form out of that silvery flow of air and light. As we drew closer, I saw that it was not a mirage, but a covered wagon, stranded and motionless in the middle of the salt pan.

I could see no sign of life or movement. The canvas sides of the wagon were rolled up and tied so as to form a strip along the top of the supporting hoops. It shaded the sun but would not keep out the breeze, if there were one, which at that moment there was not. Other than the shimmering heat, the air was as still and dead as the wagon itself.

Under the hoops were heaped a ragged assortment of household furnishings, a few chests and barrels, and what seemed to be three loose piles of rags, two in the back of the wagon, and one under the driver's seat.

A third larger heap, dark and twisted, lay a few yards in front of the wagon, and it was with some difficulty that I recognized it as the remains of a flesh-horse, dead where it had fallen. Now, though it did not seem long dead, it was little more than a pile of bones held together by hide, the legs jutting out at odd angles, the neck and head drawn back grotesquely. It must have been near starvation when it died, and it was a miracle it had dragged this wagon so far into the wasteland.

I drew Piston to a stop, and sat there surveying this sad tableau of mortality. Though I had hoped to find the absence of flesh-men here, I had no wish of their harm, and no notion that this harsh place's name would take on such literal meaning.

I was about to check the wagon for bodies when the bundle of rags under the driver's seat began to stir. A flap of cloth was thrown back, and I saw a man's arm, then his hat and head emerge from the rags. He stared at me, his eyes white circles in the dark shadows under his hat brim. He blinked and shook his head, as though I might be a dream.

"Bess," he said finally, "daddy, wake up. There is—someone—here!" His voice was raspy and cracked like dried salt. He tilted his head, as though trying to get a better look at me. "What manner of man are you, stranger?"

I was used to this. There were still few mechanical men such as myself this far west. "I am called Liberty Brass. I am a Brass Artilleryman, late of the Confederate Army, now a freeman courtesy of the late President Lincoln. I have been a hand, a cowpoke, and many other things, but today I am just a traveler. I journey west across this valley to the town of Darwin, which I believe to be the nearest inhabited place to here."

Slowly, timidly, a second bundle of rags uncovered itself, and I saw a woman, thin-faced, with long hair the color of corn-silk. Her cheeks looked sunken, and her eyes were recessed deep in dark sockets, which I had learned was often a sign of ill-health in flesh-men. But she still smiled at me, and lifted a smaller bundle to her chest, one that moved, weakly waving tiny arms and legs. "You're a wind-up man," she said, her voice as thin and frail as her frame.

I tipped my hat. "I am, ma'am."

The man slid from under the bench and stood himself up. His face was thin and covered with a thin, sun-bleached, beard. He was also thin, but tall and with some width on his shoulders, and hands that had long known hard work. His pants were worn, patched at the knees, and his shirt hung in tatters, the sleeves ripped off to expose his wiry arms. I am a poor judge of human age, but he seemed young to have a wife and child, and yet I judged that to be the situation. He had called to his "daddy," but the last bundle in the wagon did not stir.

"If that is what you are," said the man, "then the good Lord is making angels out of metal, for that is surely what you are to us! My father is old and sick," the man said, "and my wife is also ill and weak from lack of water. Our horse died two days ago, our food is nearly out, and our water barrel is near empty as well."

He looked around, and seemed like he had forgotten something important. "Forgive me. My name is Eli Adamson, and this is my wife Bess, and my baby boy. We travel west to meet my cousin Abraham in California, where we seek our fortune. My father is named Ezekiel Adamson, but I fear he is in no condition to greet you. His fever is most dire."

"You are in need of help," I said, "and I would be glad to aid you if I can. I judge that if I ride hard, I might get to Darwin in a day, get my horse and I wound, and bring back water and food, with help from the town sure to follow."

The man frowned. "That will not do." He said. "That will not do at all."

I tilted my head, confused. "I judge that to be the best course," I said. "If you wish, I can take you with me, though it will be a hard ride, and the weight of you may slow even Piston down a bit."

He shook his head. "I could not leave my family. My wife and father are ill and need my care. I would not abandon them to this place, and I would never leave my son here."

"Then let me go for help," I said.

"No," he said. "The Lord has delivered your great mechanical horse to us, and it is obvious that he could pull our wagon and our entire party."

I could not argue that point. Piston was built as a war-horse, to pull wagons of ammunition and gun carriages. He would have no trouble with this wagon. But then we would move only a fraction of the speed. Our journey would take days, and if Piston's spring unwound too fast, we might not make it at all.

But though I had been emancipated in law, I had been born into the servitude of men, and I was still not accustomed to contradicting the wishes of a flesh-man without good cause. At that moment of uncertainty, the cause did not seem great, and thus our great misfortune did begin.

With some difficulty the man Adamson and I were able to

harness Piston to the wagon. The collar barely fit over his head, and had to be placed carefully so as not to damage the delicate brass horns of his ears. The harness straps were too short for his great girth, and we had to improvise their extension with rope and leather straps from the wagon. As we did our work, he kept looking at me with his great glass eyes, as though even he sensed the lack of wisdom in our actions.

But soon enough the task was done, and given that Piston was immune to heat, we immediately got under way. Adamson started to climb into the seat to drive the wagon, but I assured him there was no need. Piston would drive himself, and I could stop or direct him with the sound of my voice. I urged the man to rest and hide himself from the sun for the rest of the day. But he insisted on sitting in the seat, even if there was no purpose to it.

As for me, it was desirable that I ride the wagon to preserve my own winding, but I could not sit on the seat without collapsing it under the weight of my metal frame. Instead, I simply crouched down in the front of the wagon. Sitting is of little use to a clockwork man, and kneeling caused my metal legs no discomfort, even if I remained so for hours.

The man spoke little, and when he did, it seemed to cause him discomfort. He took water from their dwindling supply only in small sips, reserving most of it for his family. But there was little enough even for them, and as the hours passed in the relentless sun, I watched them wilt like prairie grass before a fire. I never heard the old man speak, but on occasion he would break into spasms of coughing that seemed to cause the woman great concern.

It was with special curiosity that I observed the child. I have never spent much time in the company of small humans, and the idea that flesh men must grow, year-by-year, from seed, is a strange one to me. This one was tiny, and seemingly completely helpless. The woman had to hold and tend it constantly, and at one point I observed her feeding it from the bumps that flesh-women have on their chests. When she noticed me watching, she seemed disturbed and pulled a tarp over herself. I looked away, uncertain how I had caused offense, but there was little point in asking. She spoke even less than the man.

At last the sun slipped behind the distant hills, and though I could not tell, I imagined it would be come cooler. My eyes are less able to see in the dark than a flesh-man's, but fortunately Piston was less limited in this regard, and he continued on, sure of foot and purpose.

I knew the moon should rise in a few hours, and with luck we could roll on the night through.

But at that moment I heard the woman speak. "Eli, your father is with the Lord now."

I was confused by her phrase, and I looked back. Near as I could tell, the elder Adamson still lay in the back of the wagon, and other than his family, he was alone.

But Eli Adamson gasped and sprang into the back of the wagon, sweeping his father into his arms. To my great surprise, he began to sob and wail, and the woman leaned on him for comfort. It was only then that I understood that the old man had died.

Uncertain what to do, I called for Piston to stop.

Though I was saddened by the man's death and the distress of the Adamsons, the ways of men were alien to me, and I did not much know how to comfort them. My words of regret seemed empty and impotent, and after a while, I decided it was time to continue on.

I turned to urge Piston forward again, but Adamson called for me to stop. "We have to bury my father," he said.

"It would be better to carry on," I said, "while the night is cool and you still have water."

"We can't continue on with a body in the wagon," he said. "There is a child here. He must be buried."

"Then I will help you remove him from the wagon. We can come back to bury him once you have water and food and your family is safe."

"And leave him for the vultures and coyotes? Never!"

I had seen no vultures or coyotes, and hardly even a lizard or snake in this desolate place, but I did not say it. Instead I helped Adamson take his father's body, wrap it in canvas, and set it on the ground. I realized as we redressed him for burial, that I had never seen his face in life. Now it was a mask in the moonlight; sunken eyes, lips pulled back from discolored teeth, a fringe of salt-and-pepper beard.

Adamson produced a shovel, but it proved ineffective in the hard ground, and we spent a good part of the night, and all of the remaining moonlight, moving stones to create a cairn to cover the body. When we were finished, Eli Adamson removed a leather-bound book from the wagon, though it was too dark for even a human to read it, and clutched it to his chest. He helped the woman down from the wagon, and together, her with the baby in her arms, they stood before the stones. I stood with them, removing my hat out of respect, but uncertain what to do.

It seemed he had the book memorized, for he recited a long passage from it, which to my surprise included the line, "though I walk through the valley of the shadow of death—" Finally he finished, and used his own words. "Oh Lord, take into your bosom your faithful servant Ezekiel. His road was long and hard, but by your decree, it ends here. May he finally know comfort and plenty in Heaven, where he will wait for our inevitable reunion. Blessed be thy name. Amen."

I realized the book was a "Bible," something some flesh-men attached importance to in a way I found hard to understand. I found it curious that flesh-men believed their creator to be some unseen but all-seeing spirit, and that they loved Him so. I wondered, if they really knew their creator as well as clockwork men knew theirs, would they be so unreserved in their affections?

By then it was too dark to continue on, and we had to hunker down and wait for the first light of the sun to show us our way.

We moved as soon as the sky was light enough to show the way, but the sun was not long to show itself over the distant mountains. We were on the alkali lake now, blinding white and flat as a boarding-house dinner table. With the light I could see now that we could have continued through the night with little trouble, steering by the stars like a sailing ship. There was nothing ahead to hinder our steps for miles, and there was little to do but stare at the mountains ahead, which seemed never to get any closer.

As I said, I cannot feel the heat, but I can see it, and I saw it in the growing deterioration of my meat-and-bone companions. I saw it in their red and peeling skin, the cracking of their lips as they turned white and flaked away like scabs, and the growing desperation in their eyes. Sometimes I would see the man and woman holding hands, their fingers clenched together as though to release them would be to drown.

The baby grew restless, his cries weak and raspy. The woman no longer thought to hide herself as she tried to feed him, but he seemed to get no nourishment from it, and I wondered if that well, too, had run dry.

The sun was high in the sky when Eli Adamson looked up with a start and stared into the distance. "Did you see it?" He asked.

I saw nothing but white salt and rock mountains, and said so.

He pointed to the northwest. "Up on that mountainside! I saw a flash! There must be people up there!"

I looked doubtfully at the hill. In daylight, my eyes are better than a man's at a distance, but I saw little sign of habitation, just a small streak of discoloration on a slope that might be tailings from a mine, or just another natural variation in the color and texture of the rocks. And the peak was well north of the land-marks I had been given to find the pass through to Darwin.

But as we pressed on, his eyes were still drawn to the distant peak. "There!" He said. "I saw it again. They can see us from their vantage point. We must stand out on the salt like a fly on sugar! They see us, and they signal us to come to them. They will have water to share!"

I expressed my doubts, but he refused to let go of the idea. "The Lord has sent us this sign! As he sent us you and your horse in our time of need, so does he send us these hospitable strangers on the mount. We must go to them!"

And so, with some reluctance, I steered Piston to the northwest.

We left the salt in the afternoon and the going became rougher, as the wagon bounced over rocks and rough ground. In time I saw the flashing too, sometimes two or three flashes in a row, and it did have the look of a signal, as someone with a shaving mirror might make.

Perhaps the man was right, I thought hopefully. Perhaps there *was* water there.

The mountainside ahead was rough and crumpled like a discarded sheet of paper, and we followed some old wagon tracks that we hoped might lead us to the mine, if that was what it was. But the trail looked wind-worn and unused, and more so as we climbed higher. My doubts returned, and brought with them hale companions.

The path, such as it was, grew narrow and steep, and I begged the man to let me unhitch Piston and ride ahead to scout. But he would have no delay. "We will stay together and keep moving!" He cried.

Finally, the road was too steep for even Piston's great strength, and the man and I got out of the wagon to lighten his load, and finally to push, grabbing the spokes of the wheel and rolling it forward, foot-by-foot. But it was not the slope of the path which was to end our progress.

I stood on the down-slope side of the wagon, and as I shifted my grip on the front wheel, there was a rumble and the dry earth began to crumble away under my feet.

I staggered back, just in time to see the back wheel of the wagon sliding down in a flow of shifting rock and dirt. I ducked down as the wagon slid right over me, sideways and tail-first over the edge.

As the far side of it cleared my head and I looked up expecting to see open sky, I instead saw the woman and her child, diving away from the plummeting wagon.

Fearing for their lives, I sprang into action, my artillery-man's brain instantly calculating the trajectory of their flight as it would the arc of a cannonball. I managed to catch them before they crashed into the unyielding rock, softening their landing with the springs built into my limbs. The woman cried out though, as her stomach folded across the metal of my arm, and I wished, just once, that I had been constructed of softer stuff.

I feared for a moment that the wagon would plummet clear down the steep mountainside, taking Piston with it. But a large boulder blocked the wagon's progress. The back wheels and axle crashed into it, splintering one wheel and crushing the back of the wagon like a matchbox.

I looked up to see the man, who had rushed to his wife and child, and the three of them huddled together there in the middle of the little wagon path. The woman sobbed. The child made little hacking cries. The man's eyes were fixed wide open, looking into nothing.

I stood and glanced up the mountain, something I had not

done in a while, and a terrible sight awaited me there. "I see it," I said.

"What?" said the woman weakly, her voice pained and full of dread. "What do you see?"

"The source of the flashes," I said.

"I see nothing," said the man, standing and looking up.

"My eyes are sharp as a hawk, and I tell you, I can see it. There was a mine there once. I can see the tailings, and a few uprights with boards attached that might have once been a miner's shack, but there has been no one there for many years, I am sure."

The man scowled at me, and if there had been enough water in his body, there might have been tears in his eyes. "Then who made those flashes? Who lured us into this dreadful fate?"

I knew the name to answer, but I did not say it. "On one of those upright timbers, some old whisky bottles hang from a bit of twine. When the wind shifts them, they catch the sun. It is nothing but the wind."

————

We unhitched Piston from what was left of the wagon. Though Eli Adamson seemed reluctant, I convinced him we should leave all their belongings behind. He took only a few things that he could keep on his person from the wreck of his wagon; his Bible, and when he thought nobody was looking, he slipped a small pistol from a wooden box and tucked it into his boot where it could be hidden by his pants leg.

I was more concerned though, about the winding of Piston's spring, and mine. I could feel the weakness of my wind, and as I gazed through the little mica sight-glass in front of Piston's saddle, I could see his great mainspring was nearly as loose as I have ever seen it.

Now perhaps you think a clockwork man is like a clock or child's toy that runs down and can simply be rewound. But that is not true for beings such as Piston and me.

It is said our minds run on sound, a song inside our heads made with resonance pipes and tiny tuning forks. If our springs ever run down, the song ends.

It dies.

If we are rewound, sometimes the body may restart, but with a mind more blank and empty than any child. To lose our winding completely was death.

But I would have to walk now, and the man and woman were barely able to move themselves, much less wind us. Piston would have to share some of his winding with me if we were to go on. He is equipped with a fitting on the side of his neck that connects to his mainspring and can engage my winding key, transferring power from his much larger spring to my smaller one.

I stood there for a moment, leaning back against my horse, feeling both relief and regret as my spring wound tighter. It was a small thing, but it felt like I was stealing the life from my beloved horse to preserve my own.

As soon as I dared, long before my spring was half-wound, I pulled away. Even if I had not considered Piston precious, we needed him to haul the woman, who seemed to grow weaker by the moment.

If there had been proper wind, and more time, Piston could have eventually rewound himself, and in turn, me, but my flesh companions had no time. Their life dwindled before my eyes.

As we prepared to leave, only one thing seemed missing. I told Adamson to get the water cask so I could lash it to Piston's side. He only shook his head sadly.

"The cask was dashed on the rocks. Our water is lost."

The man took the saddle and held the woman, who otherwise would have fallen. I walked, and because her arms had become too weak, the task of carrying the child soon fell to me. I looked down at the feeble bundle of life, and wondered that it might someday grow to be a full-sized flesh man. I wondered if it would remember me, its strange nursemaid, in this terrible time, in this terrible place.

We had to backtrack all the way to the salt flats and turn south to make the pass, as darkness fell. The moon returned, but it was often hidden behind the jagged peaks, and rarely cast its light into the pass. We moved in fits and starts as light permitted, and it was during one of those pauses that, in the darkness, I heard the man begin to weep.

I knew what must have happened, but I said nothing. I just held the child, and felt its weak stirrings in my arms.

At dawn we began to gather stones to bury the woman. He was too weak to move but the smallest ones, and I tried to conserve my spring, and so it was a poor burial that barely covered her. If the coyotes wished to feast, there would be little to stop them.

The man seemed beyond caring.

He stood at the foot of the grave, the Bible clutched to his chest, but words did not seem to come. After a while, he finally said, "Lord, I have no words for you right now." Then he tenderly placed the holy book on top of the cairn over the woman's heart. "May it offer you some comfort, my darling."

He and I were both able to ride Piston then, the baby again safely in his arms. But we had not gone another quarter mile before my wonderful horse began to falter. He traveled another few hundred yards before his front legs gave out. He knelt down and seemed to freeze.

I leapt down, and was relieved as he turned his head slowly toward me and he followed me with his big glass eyes. He slowly settled down into his belly, his legs folded under him. I placed my hand on his nose and he moved against it weakly. "You wait here, good friend. You wait here and I'll be back soon with help to wind your spring up real tight. Mark my word!"

But I did not know. I did not know if any of us would survive.

Before I left, I opened his saddle and set up the little windmill. The air was still, but perhaps some breeze might make its way down the canyon, enough to keep my faithful steed alive until I could return.

Finally he lay his head down and shuttered his eyes, only the slight twitching of his ears to tell me he still lived. Clockwork beings such as us do not sleep, but we can shut ourselves down, using just enough of our spring to keep our minds humming, to keep the song barely playing in our heads.

With a fully wound spring, we can stay like that for days, or even months, but as exhausted as Piston's spring was, if a single cog stalled, a single bearing bound up with a bit of grit, it could end in an instant. He might last a day or two as he was, but I could not count on it. I left him behind, uncertain if I would ever see him again.

And so we continued on, the man and I and the babe-in-arms. At first, Adamson carried the child, but soon he was too weak, and after he stumbled and fell, barely turning to avoid falling on the infant, I took that small burden back.

I walked slowly, but the man kept falling behind, stumbling and staggering, and stopping; to catch his breath, or gather his resolve, I could never be sure.

"I'm holding you back, tin man. Slowing you down." Behind me, I heard the slide of steel on leather, and the cocking of a gun.

It took a moment for my dulled mind to figure it out, and I was too slow.

"Some say suicide is a sin, but they have never walked in my boots."

I turned in time to see him put the barrel of the gun in his mouth.

A sharp crack echoed off the distant hills.

A red flower bloomed on the dry earth behind him, and he fell.

There would be no cairn of stones for him, no time of prayer. But I was sure now, he would not wish it. He had given all he had left for the small bundle in my arms, and I could not fail him.

All that was left to do was walk, one foot in front of the other, up the pass, with nothing to do but think. Nothing to do but doubt.

Would my spring hold out? Had I interpreted the landmarks right? Was this even the right pass?

There was no going back, even if I ran into a dead-end canyon around the next bend. My spring would not hold out to get me back down and try again.

It was forward or nothing.

The rock pinnacles around me offered some protection from the sun, but when it did show itself, I shaded the child with my body, even walking sideways for a while, and hoping my metal hide didn't become so hot itself to add to his suffering.

I realized I had never learned the child's given name, and now I might never know. If I brought him out of this wilderness, it would be as if he were born again, and whoever took him would give him a new name.

I thought of that, and it made me sad, that his parents had given their all to him, to be forgotten as though they had never existed. But there was one name I did know. "Adamson," I said to him. "If they ask me your name, I will tell them it is Adamson."

For a clockwork man, to feel one's spring fully unwinding is a terrible thing. To be truthful, after the terrible horrors of Gettysburg, when I had contemplated letting my spring run down and end my miserable existence, I had almost let that happen, come dreadfully close to that silent abyss. But I had decided that dark night that I wished to live, so it was with a special dread that I marched on, knowing what was coming. As the spring grew slack, it became unsteady and undependable, too weak to drive the higher functions, the mind, and the eyes.

My thoughts dulled, and time seemed to drag along. My arms grew numb, and I could barely see far enough to look down occasionally to be sure I had not dropped my precious parcel. Sometimes my thoughts would seem to fade away completely, and I would snap back to awareness, the terrain beneath my feet completely different.

But had I traveled a yard or a mile? I could not be certain.

One foot in front of the other. On and on.

Then, in front of me, I saw something dark in white sand. At first it was just a dot, and I thought it a rock, steering toward it so I did not simply walk in circles given my weakness and confusion.

But it was not a rock. It was a man-made thing, round, painted, but gleaming of tin where the paint had chipped away. Something like a snake curled next to it, and as I drew closer, I saw that it was a leather strap.

It was then I realized what the thing was, a familiar object I had seen countless times on the battlefields of a now-distant war. A canteen, a hollow disk of metal made to contain water.

I hastened my pace, though I could feel the weak spring in my chest slacken with each step. I fell to my knees before the thing and set my burden gently on the soft sand, reaching eagerly for the canteen. But as I did, I saw the stopper hanging free on its leather cord.

Still, I maintained a shred of hope as I shook it and felt something heavy shift within. But as I turned it, I heard not the slosh of water, but another sound. I upended the canteen, and a stream of dust flowed forth, feeding small clouds of despair to the wind. No life-giving fluid here. No cool elixir to momentarily relieve the madness of the desert. Only the sad illustration of things that might have been: how a drink of water might have saved a flesh-man's life. Or two. Or three.

I threw the canteen aside and struggled to my feet. After a moment's hesitation, I bent to pick up my small burden. The baby did not move, and its weight seemed to me like a boulder. I knew the reasonable thing would have been to leave it there. To save myself if I could, faint hope there even was of that.

There had been so many chances to do the reasonable thing, and I had failed at each of them, failed to resist the will of my flesh and blood companions. Of those, I had some regrets, but not of this one. If I had learned nothing in this valley of death, it was that all thinking beings, of flesh and metal, we are all prisoners of our own folly, and have but to see it through.

One foot in front of the other. On and on.

In a moment of confusion I imagined myself as an angel, with wings of filigreed gold, and I made what for me passes as a laugh, amused at such a thought.

I looked down at the burden that I carried and imagined myself, for just a moment, as an agent of an unseen force, sent to save him. And strangely it gave me some small comfort as my mind drifted further into the fog.

One foot in front of another.

Tick. Tick. Tick.

I am a clockwork man, a thing of springs and metal and gears.

One foot in front of another. Like a machine.

That is all I am. A machine.

And then the machine stopped.

I felt a jarring. I heard a clang of metal against stone.

"What in hell!" The voice seemed to come from far away. "It's a tin man, walked out of the desert!"

My mind came into focus for a moment, like a slide in a lantern show, and I could see a street, wooden buildings, and people coming from every direction. I looked down at my burden.

So still.

Another voice. "What he got there?"

The burden was lifted from me, and I stared down at my empty arms. My head would not move. My vision faded, and I fell over on my side, laying in the dirt. Then I could not even feel that.

I could only hear.

"Lord in heaven, it's a baby!"

"Is it—"

"It's alive! Fetch water, and get the child to the doc."

I thought I heard someone kneel in the dirt next to me. "He saved him. That tin man saved him!"

"Right out of the desert!"

"It needs winding, if it ain't dead already!"

I heard a voice quite close to my ear. "Metal man, what do you need?"

I wondered if I had the strength to speak, and to my surprise, I did.

"Please, sir," I implored, "go wind my horse."

A GOOD NEGRO

EZEKIEL JAMES BOSTON

Ezekiel James Boston lives in Las Vegas, my new hometown. He has sold stories all over the place and I am proud to say will have another great story coming up in another anthology I edited for Fiction River.

This powerful original story takes place in Ezekiel's dark fantasy Otherside of Elsewhere universe, of which he has two new releases.

What makes Ezekiel perfect to write Pulphouse *stories is that he has no fear of writing about subjects that others in this new world would run screaming from. His skill and his courage are why I hope to have many more Ezekiel James Boston stories in these pages.*

———

Some things are worth dying for. Curious Negro's father had told him that, but he never understood it—never felt it—until that day when he found the edge between the black and white world as he knew it and the perception altering world of the creator.

Beyond the edge of the panel that bordered the town and the world of Good Ol' Days, the creator's world had…

Curious struggled to find a word for it.

Depth.

That's the word his old grade school teacher Smart Negro used when describing the introspective feeling that you got from a good book. But this kind of depth was more like one of Uppity Negro's underground pamphlets. The ones that guessed at there being something beyond Good Ol' Days. A *third dimension*. One where the world wasn't only made from black ink.

The creator's world was no longer a theory on some leaflets that Curious kept hidden under his bed. It was real and made from inks other than black. Inks he didn't have words for. The new inks made Curious feel depth when he hoisted himself up onto the edge of the panel and peered out into the creator's room.

On a basic level, the creator's room looked like Curious's own dormitory with a messy full-sized bed piled high with dark covers next to a small desk cluttered with schoolwork. While Curious's walls were mostly as bare as his earthen floor, the opposite wall had posters of bands, mostly men with guitars and long hair. The flooring was hardwood panels.

A large light-filled window was to the left. Where Curious's room had one pennant above the window, the creator had two: *USV*, and *University of Southern Virginia*. Curious couldn't help but wonder, if there was a way to get there—other than going over the panel's edge—how far would USV be from his own Nigger U.

The delicious smell of fried chicken filled the air.

There were no curvy scent lines indicating where the chicken rested in the room to show him where the smell was coming from. The smell was just there. Hanging in the air. Same for the heat in the room. He could see the light from the window, but there weren't any wavy heat-lines to indicate the toasty warmth on his face, neck, and chest. In his world, there'd been two or more lines showing the heat source.

The sound of a vacuum cleaner turned Curious's attention to the south.

No sound clouds.

No onomatopoeias to indicate what he should be hearing. Just, the sound of a vacuum being run beyond the dormitory door. A door that looked like it locked on the inside.

Curious froze. Dread seized his stomach.

Only Pures had locks on the inside of their doors. They were able to lock the world out and feel safe from one another where the Negros were always locked in well before sundown; and usually right after school or work.

Curious had seen the creator's quill a few times in his life. The shaft was black like him. Part of the brush was not-colored—like the Pures—but the ink it held was always as black as Curious. Because of that, he had imagined the creator was a Negro like himself. However, being able to lock the door signaled that the creator was a Pure.

The realization made Curious want to drop back down into the panel, climb down the highest tree in the forest, and pretend he hadn't discovered the creator's world.

A feeble moan. "Hel—" Came from the bed.

Curious glanced to the pile of covers. Was someone under them?

Another soft word. "Hel—" Came from near the far corner of the bed.

There wasn't a dialogue balloon. Like the sound from the vacuum and smell of the fried chicken, the word went through the air without any indication that it truly existed.

"Hel— 'leeze."

That sounded like *help please.*

As much as Curious just wanted to go back to his dorm and forget about this, he took a deep breath and used the edge of the panel to haul himself all the way out.

Standing on the creator's desk, in the creator's world, the room grew in size.

Curious gawked at the soda cans on the desk that were two times taller than him. He was used to things being small in the distance and growing in size as he got closer to them, but these cans...they all seemed to be the same height. Just at different distances away.

And they stayed the same height as he walked between them to the bed.

The sound of the vacuum cleaner faded as it moved further away.

Feeble sobs came from the same corner of the bed.

Going toward the sound, Curious stepped onto the long, hilly field of soft dark covers.

The closer he got, the more anxiousness built. When he'd

heard similar in the past, he'd always come across a Negro that the Pures had punished for breaking a law that only applied to Negros.

Curious had seen some real messes in the past. Negros beaten so bad that they were barely more than scraggly blots of ink with abstract expressions above them indicating just how bad off they were. Those other times, he'd at least been able to see the squiggles, pound signs, and broken stars as he approached to mentally prepare himself for what he was about to see.

The creator's world didn't provide such indicators.

Up near the top, the cover-hills undulated slightly. Near the crest of the last hill, Curious crouched and leaned to peer over the edge.

———

Curious hadn't always been curious. Like many boys and girls he had grown up with, he was just another Negro. He and his friends would often head out on some whacky adventure. The days were almost always warm and sunny, and they'd laugh about their hijinks when safely back home on their porch, eating watermelon and spitting seeds. Life was much simpler before he earned a name.

He and his friends were playing *hide and find a nigger* in the forest when he had come across a shoe. All by itself. In the forest. Then he found another just below feet dangling in the air at eye height.

Above him, Uppity had been hung by his neck from a tree. Each of his eyes were now an X.

Curious had run home, told his father, and led his father to where Uppity hung.

Looking over the edge of the cover felt just like taking his

74

father to Uppity's body. Being compelled to do something that he didn't want to do. To see something that he didn't want to see.

The fried chicken smell was stronger up here.

Down below was a huge dark-skinned head—three or four times bigger than his whole body—on a pillow.

Curious turned back to the field of covers for a moment. He guessed that what he thought were hills was the rest of this giant's body.

The giant's eyes were closed. It wept weakly as tiny tears pooled on the inside corners of its upper eye and thin streams ran down the side of its face. Its enormous mouth was held wide open by some kind of device at the corners of its mouth that did the opposite job of what a clamp would do. The device looked like it was hard and had a loop that hung past the chin. Curious could see all of the giant's terribly huge teeth and massive tongue. Its breath was funky.

While the size of the giant's nose, lips, forehead, and ears were of smaller proportions, Curious couldn't help but see himself in the giant face. If not himself, then surely one of the many Negros that he knew.

A plate of giant-sized fried chicken, a thigh and two drum-sticks—one with a bite from it—was right next to the giant's head. A fork was in the corn niblets and a spoon in the gravy-laden mashed potatoes.

Curious asked, "How can I help you, giant?"

The giant's eyes sprung open. They lit on Curious, flicked toward his speech bubble, and then focused on Curious again.

Silent and wide-eyed, the giant stared at him.

Curious glanced to the far edge of the bed in the corner in case another Negro had gotten out of the panel before him and was stuck there.

Nothing.

Curious focused on the giant. "Were you calling for help?"

The giant blinked. Closed its eyes tight. And opened them again to look at Curious.

"Yu 'ot 'eal."

Curious stated "Yes I am. I'm as real as you. My name is Curious Negro." More than before, he wanted to run away, but stayed. If the giant rose in anger, he wasn't sure if he could make it back to the panel, but he'd sure try.

Curious asked, "Why do you have that thing in your mouth? It makes you hard to understand."

The giant closed its eyes tight again and shook its head.

Though it clearly didn't believe Curious was there, it didn't get up or bat him away. Equally as clear, it looked to be as distressed as a bear stuck in a trap.

Curious slid down the giant's blanketed shoulder and leapt onto the bed. He went to the plate, grabbed onto the spoon handle, and tried pulling it. It was heavy. The potatoes on it made it even heavier.

He walked to the fork and took a moment to summon his Negro strength. He spat on each of his hands, rubbed them together, and took ahold of the fork. With a mighty heave, the fork scraped the plate as he pulled it onto the bed.

The giant said, "Holy 'hit. Yu ar' 'eal."

"Yup." Curious pulled the fork onto the blanket. Some niblets came with it, but, step by step, Curious walked backward pulling the fork up the blanket. His shoulders burned, his back ached, and his legs were sore. Still. He dug deep and got the fork to the top of the hill.

All the while, the giant tried to talk to him, but Curious couldn't make sense of most of what it was saying. Part of it sounded like it was trying to say that it made him, but that was ridiculous. The creator just had to be a Pure. There were too many indicators.

Curious stopped and sat for a quick rest. He could really go for some lemonade or punch right now.

There had been times when Curious and his friends were caught stealing watermelons by Farmer Dave Pure. After a good tanning, Farmer Dave would make them work the fields through day and night to make more melons grow the next day.

The break he took was no more than what Farmer Dave allowed.

Curious got back to his feet, wiped his brow, and spat on his hands again. He took a hold of the fork by the tines and eased the handle down into the loop of the thing holding the giant's mouth open. Once it was in place, he held onto the tines and jumped off the hill.

The giant's chin turned the fork into a lever and yanked the contraption from the giant's mouth.

Curious tumbled down the giant's neck.

Tines first, the fork came down at him.

Curious dodged the fork. But he didn't see the contraption coming.

It landed on him. Worse, the fork fell on top of it; pinning his back, left shoulder, and left arm flat against the bed.

Curious tried to pull himself free with his right arm. Nothing doing.

He pushed up against the weight, but it was way too heavy. And with one of his arms trapped, he couldn't spit on his hands and rub them together to summon his Negro strength.

He was stuck. And, as soon as a Pure saw him, they would say that the jig was up.

And it would be.

————

In Good Ol' Days, getting caught doing wrong by another Negro usually meant getting the strap. Being caught by a Pure meant being whipped. Because of the Unbreakable Jim Crow laws passed, the Pures rarely had to kill Negros anymore. Not because the Pures would shy away from killing, but because any Negro that wanted to stay alive had learned not to test the law.

At least, not to break the deadly ones like—outside of going to work or going home—being on the Pure side of town, using anything reserved for Pures, and—the worst—lusting after a Pure.

Uppity was the last Negro Curious knew who had been killed for breaking the law, and the Negro's eyes had been X'd out.

Curious had always wondered what law Uppity had undermined, but no one knew and would shush Curious when he asked. Curious hadn't stopped asking, but his fellow Negros ignored the question and started calling him curious.

Given how the Pures were in Good Ol' Days, Curious trembled at the thought of what a giant creator-Pure would do.

Gritting his teeth, Curious dug his fingers into the blanket and pulled. Nothing.

The giant said, "Thank you. Can. You get. To the. Phone. And dial, 9-1-1?"

"No. I'm stuck." Curious struggled against the weight again without any gain. "The thing that was in your mouth is on me."

"The cheek. Retractor. Fell. On you?"

Curious shrugged the shoulder he could. "If that's what you call it. Yes."

The giant began to rock the bed.

One of the loose niblets landed wet and buttery against Curious's cheek. He kept pushing it away, but the giant's movement kept rocking it back into his face.

About to complain, the fork fell off of the cheek retractor and onto his lower back.

Curious pushed up against the retractor. It slid slimily off of his back. His left arm was free.

He spat on his hands, rubbed them together, and dug both hands into the blanket.

Curious yanked and bucked.

The cover pulled from the corner a touch, but he had enough resistance to get the weight of the fork from his back, over his butt, and down onto the back of his thighs.

He pushed up to his hands and knees, and the fork tumbled down his legs with the curve arched over his legs.

"I'm free." Curious got to his feet and looked at the giant.

The giant was moving its jaw side to side and swallowing. Curious had never kept his mouth open for a long time, but he imagined how it would dry the mouth out.

Curious prompted, "You said 9-1-1?" And asked, "What city? Oh, and I'll need the other two numbers."

"Huh?" The giant's voice was still weak. "What?"

Curious said, "To dial. You know, city plus five digits?" His mind went to how he was going to actually call. "I mean, I'll try calling, but it's going to be a dag gum huge chore to get one of your giant nickels to a phone booth, but I'll try." Concern about over committing brought a question to his mind. "How far is it to the closest Negro phone booth?"

The giant's gaze went past Curious. "Use. That one." It raised its chin to motion across the room.

Curious turned. There were gaps in the posters on the wall and in one of the gaps was a phone. An actual phone in a bedroom. It looked much smaller than the ones he'd seen and way futuristic, and had three rows of four buttons instead of a rotary.

If the lock on the inside of the door wasn't a big enough clue that the creator was a Pure, that sci-fi feature phone cemented it.

For a split second, he wondered how he would even get up there to use it.

Then Curious's better judgment kicked in. He said, "I can't use that one."

"Why? Not?"

"It's not for Negros." Curious pointed to the poster where the *nigger phone* sign would've been if Negros were allowed to use it.

Still pointing, he faced the giant. "There's no sign."

A pitied expression washed over the giant's face. Not a look that it was asking to be pitied, but one that made Curious feel like it pitied him.

The giant said, "Those. Rules…Are. Gone." It swallowed. "Call 9-1-1."

Curious shook his head. Using a Pure's phone wasn't normally a death sentence, but in the creator's fancy place, it very well could be.

He pointed at the giant. "You call."

"Can't." The giant sighed. "I'm tied. Up."

"Tied up?" Curious moved to the headboard to make sure the bed was really just a bed and not some sort of newfangled combination of a bed and whipping post. While he did see where ropes were anchored to the wall beyond the pillow, there wasn't a post to be found. The only time Negros were tied up in Good Ol' Days was when they were going to be whipped, and that never happened on a bed.

Curious returned to where he had stood. He asked, "Why are you tied to a bed?"

The pitied expression broke as the giant's eyes started to water and its lips trembled. "Race play."

"Race play?" Curious frowned. He couldn't find the connection between the two words that would make it, or this situation, make sense. However, he understood *play*. He asked, "What's that? Is it a game?"

"Sort of. Please." The giant begged. "Call 9-1-1."

Curious's heart ached for the giant. It didn't want to be tied up, but there was no way he was going to pick up a Pure's phone.

He snapped his fingers.

The solution was obvious. Curious would just untie the giant and let it get in trouble. He might get a few lashes for helping, but nothing like what the giant would get for actually using the phone.

"Don't cry." Curious winked at the giant. "I'll have you free in a jiffy." Chest puffed with pride, he set off back to the headboard with a determined stride.

———

No matter how much Curious spat on his hands and rubbed them together, he couldn't get any of the ropes to release. He even tried working the actual knot, but the creator must've been a sailor because those things didn't budge an inch.

Ego deflated and tired to the bone from trying, he walked back into the giant's view.

The giant's slight hopeful expression shattered into a thousand defeated pieces. It closed its eyes and wept.

Curious went to the plate of food hoping to find a flake of spinach. Eating replenished Negro stamina—watermelon was the best—but eating spinach also made them as strong as five.

There was no spinach or leafy vegetable.

The smell was too much for Curious and he stole a bite of the chicken. It pushed at the back of his throat. Warm and juicy. As he swallowed, the weariness fell away from his body and his stomach bulged.

Amazed, he blinked at it. When he had been in the panel, he'd eat enough that he felt the way he now looked.

The bulge went flat.

He took another bite and wiped his mouth with the back of his hand; he didn't want the giant to see him taking a small break and eating. He watched the bulge grow in his stomach, stay for a moment, and then go flat again.

Another idea hit him. He swallowed and asked, "How about I feed you. That should give you strength."

Lips tight, the giant shook its head in dismay. "Please. Make the. Phone call." The giant was gaining a little strength. Enough to speak more than a single word at a time, but the volume of its voice was still quite low.

It said, "Curious. Be. Good. Negro."

Curious felt a slight change inside. His hallmark trait, his curiosity, diminished as his want to follow rules started to feel like a need. He looked at the phone, again.

Struggling against the command to become a good Negro, he scanned the room for a possible way to get up there. It was against the rules, but he had to make the call before the giant changing his name took over his being.

The posters. They were held in place by pushpins. If he could find something he could use for a rope—

The sound of keys jangling came from the door and the lock turned.

He dove under the blanket. It was hot, heavy, and funky.

A voice, muffled by the massive blanket, lit the air. For a moment, there was a surprised tone in the voice before it turned angry.

The bed rocked.

Curious began to army crawl deeper under the covers.

Next thing Curious knew, he was sailing through the air in a sea of blankets. It felt like he'd been loaded into a slingshot and set to sail.

He couldn't see anything besides the blanket.

Then the flying came to a sudden stop. And he and the

blanket—with its heat, weight, and funk—fell.

It was hard to breathe, but not suffocating. He could feel gravity beneath him, but had no idea which way would be the surest way out.

He started crawling.

The bends, twists, and folds of the blanket were like a maze. His mind kept telling him that he'd accidentally doubled back or turned a circle. That he'd never get out.

He ignored that feeling and kept moving.

Just as he saw a sliver of light, with a snap of the blanket, he was launched back into the air. Hard.

He hit the ceiling.

His eyes clamped shut as instincts took over.

He straightened himself out and arched his back. Curious rocked back and forth like he was on a swing that occasionally looped and would never end.

His chest brushed the hardwood flooring as momentum swung him up.

He spread out his arms and legs. And fell a small distance.

Almost under the bed, he stumbled around trying to keep his balance. The room felt like it was still rocking and threw him. He stumbled, dropped to his knees and puked drumstick shaped blotches onto the floor.

When he got his senses again, the door was closed. Beneath it, he could see trammeled carpet in the hallway and a closed door across the way.

What was he doing there?

He should've already been back in Good Ol' Days.

Distant conversation and laughter sounded like it came from down the hall, but there were no sound-lines to indicate from which direction.

He looked up to the bed.

The cover was back and, from the floor, he couldn't see if the giant was still there. What remained of his curiosity made him want to know.

He grabbed onto the covers and climbed it like a rope in PE.

The giant was there. The plate and food were gone, and the cheek retractor was back in place. Its eyes were closed and it was crying again.

Curiosity sated, he hustled down the blankets to the foot of the bed before the giant saw him. He hopped from the bed back onto the desk. As much as he wanted to help, he felt the change inside become complete.

He walked back to the panel's edge that would lead down to the tallest tree back home.

While he thought the creator was a Pure, he knew otherwise now. The bound giant was his creator because only the creator could remove his burning curiosity with nothing but a few words.

Lamenting no longer being special, he was now just another good Negro. The kind his creator inked to stay in line.

Feeling bad. Feeling like he should've done more.

Feeling like he was turning his back on his own kind. He turned away from his crying, tied-up creator.

While he still had the memory of being willing to die for discovering the creator's world, or die to stay in it, he had truly become what his creator considered to be a good Negro.

As such, he went back into the Good Ol' Days panel.

COLLECTOR'S CURSE: A DAN SHAMBLE, ZOMBIE P.I. ADVENTURE

KEVIN J. ANDERSON

As I have said a number of times, I think Kevin J. Anderson might be one the busiest writers working today, as well as one of the most prolific.

He has published more than 140 bestselling novels and with his wife, bestselling writer Rebecca Moesta, founded Wordfire Press eight years ago.

Kevin is known for Star Wars, X-Files, *and* Dune *novels, as well as his many original science fiction novels. But back in 2012 he started something a little different for him, a series of humorous horror mysteries featuring Dan Shamble, Zombie P.I.*

This is the second original Dan Shamble story in Pulphouse *and I am hoping for a lot more because a Zombie Private Eye just can't be any more perfect for* Pulphouse.

––––––

When my ghost girlfriend Sheyenne and I went to a quirky estate sale, we didn't expect to find horrific murders caused by nefarious curses. That's not what you usually encounter at estate sales, which are filled with oddities, antiques, furniture, and unusual leftovers from a person's life. At least we did find some bargains and collectibles, too.

.The estate sale tables covered the poorly maintained yard of a poorly maintained shuttered-up house in a quiet neighborhood. After all the monsters had returned to the world in the event known as the Big Uneasy, many of them eventually settled down in conventional residential areas in the Unnatural Quarter.

Eldon Muff was a crotchety, bitter old werewolf who had bought the ramshackle house in the turbulent days immediately after the Big Uneasy, when real estate prices dropped dramatically. Some might say he'd paid a song for it, but Eldon had no interest in songs, or music, or any entertainment whatsoever. He had lived alone and died alone, never married—which was no surprise at all to anyone who had ever spent more than five minutes with him. Even harpies from a paid dating service refused to go out with Eldon more than once.

Fortunately, as a zombie detective, I had never worked with Eldon, though he constantly threatened to sue anyone who had slighted him. He spouted every conspiracy meme he saw on social media (even the ones insisting that such memes were themselves a conspiracy to make people doubt conspiracy theories). My Best Human Friend, Officer Toby McGoohan, had dealt with many of Eldon's complaints though, and McGoo often stopped by our offices just to blow off steam whenever he dealt with the surly old werewolf.

Eldon had filed formal complaints against the paperboy for harassing him (by ringing his doorbell and trying to collect the months-overdue subscription), or when a young lycanthropic hooligan continually crept onto his property to urinate on the bushes, marking his territory as dogs will often do. No matter how loudly Eldon howled, "Get off my lawn!" the werewolf teenager kept coming back, clearly entertained by Eldon's impotent fury. No, the old werewolf had not made many friends.

Now that he was dead, all of his neighbors came out to pick over his possessions, looking at the display tables strewn with ridiculous and useless items, but trying to haggle down the prices nevertheless.

Sheyenne and I thought it would be a fine excuse for a date, just a zombie P.I. and a ghost out for an afternoon stroll. We enjoyed observing the curiosity seekers who picked over the jelly-jar glasses, the hideous clock in the rounded belly of a laughing Buddhist monk, a lava lamp with real lava now hardened into dull black lumps, a folding kitchen table with room enough for one, decks of playing cards that had only been used for games of solitaire, and folded clothing that exuded an "old man" smell.

"Tell me if you see anything you like, Spooky," I said.

Sheyenne's spectral brow furrowed. "Don't hold your breath."

She was far more beautiful than I deserved. As a ghost, she couldn't touch me, and our romance faced a few challenges due to intangibility, but we did our best. She had been alive when we started dating, as was I, but sometimes relationships take an unexpected turn. Today I wore my usual brown sport jacket with the clumsily stitched bullet holes across the front, and I tilted my fedora in place, though not enough to cover the bullet hole in the middle of my forehead. It was a reminder of how I'd been killed on a case.

I picked up a classic metal lunchbox from the old TV show *The Munsters*, which, after the Big Uneasy, was now viewed as an insightful family drama. Next to it were packs of *Twilight Zone* trading cards, never opened, with bubblegum petrified so hard it was beyond the ability of even a shark-jawed demon to chew. The tables were full of similar nostalgic stuff.

"Sure is a lot of junk," I said.

"Some would call them rarities and collectibles," said a frizzy-furred gremlin who bustled up, hoping she could catch my interest. I recognized Rita, a savvy gremlin businesswoman who had taken over her brother's pawn shop after his unfortunate murder. Rita was running the estate sale.

"We're just looking," I replied. "I'm not much of a collector."

"We are bargain hunters, though," Sheyenne said and moved on to another table.

Eldon Muff was more than a collector or bargain hunter, though. He'd been a hoarder, but since he kept his shades drawn and his doors locked, and never had company over, no one really understood the extent of his fervor. I couldn't imagine how all these possessions spread on table after table across the yard, filling the garage, the driveway, and the sidewalk could possibly fit inside one small rundown house, but the old werewolf must have packed every corner and every room, wall to ceiling.

Unfortunately, his overzealous collecting led to his demise. Eldon collected possessions like he collected grudges, but apparently he didn't organize either one very well. The old werewolf had been buried under a mountain of discontinued monster Hummel figurines still in their original boxes. The cute but disturbing miniature figures of charming slack-faced ghouls and rotting zombies hadn't found the right audience. Eldon had bought the whole truckload, also presumably for a song, but he had stacked the pile of original boxes too high, and they fell over and crushed him. An unknown amount of time later, the insistent young zombie paperboy had come yet again to collect on the overdue subscription fee and found him dead. The withered, half-rotted werewolf looked decidedly less cute than even the least cute of the monster Hummel figurines.

Eldon Muff had no heirs, not even any friends, but a new bulldozing company was eager to buy his house so they could use it for employee practice—hence, the reason for this complete life-liquidation sale. I hoped that at least the unpaid zombie paperboy would receive part of the proceeds for his overdue bill.

Curious, I went to a rack of shelves crammed with old paperback books, the kind with red edges and garish artwork, 50¢ cover price. They looked to be in mint condition. They caught my eye because they were detective novels, at least three dozen of them. A grin crept across my cold gray face.

"Look at these, Spooky. They're classics by John D. MacDonald. I love his detective Travis McGee." I pulled out three at random. *Nightmare in Pink, A Purple Place for Dying, Free Fall in Crimson.*

Sheyenne snuggled close, and I felt the tingling aura of her insubstantial yet curvaceous body. I said, "Reading old detective novels is what inspired me to be a private investigator. Well, that and not being able to make it through police academy." It was a constant embarrassment to know that McGoo was better at criminal academics than I was.

I called out to the gremlin running the sale. "How much are the paperbacks, Rita?"

The fuzzy woman glanced up from wrapping a complete set of Flintstones shot glasses. "Fifty cents each."

I considered, glancing at Sheyenne. "These were my favorites." I looked at the three old paperbacks, then pondered the entire collection.

"You don't have time to read, Beaux," Sheyenne reminded me. "You have too many cases."

"Maybe they'll serve as inspiration," I said, deciding to take the three, but not the whole set. Sheyenne went over to look at the varied kitchen utensils, even though as a ghost she couldn't eat, nor did she spend much time cooking. I happily paid for my three books.

As I opened the first paperback, *Nightmare in Pink,* I was surprised to discover handwriting inside. When I realized that the books were signed, I felt like a game show contestant who had unexpectedly won a bonus round. But when I flipped to the title page I discovered not John D. MacDonald's autograph, but the much-less-collectible scrawl of the old werewolf, words written in angry, hard strokes. "I hereby curse the paperboy Bobby Neumann for his incessant harassment. When this curse is activated, he shall die a truly horrible death. My vengeance extends beyond the grave! Sincerely yours, Eldon Muff."

The crotchety werewolf sure did know how to hold a grudge. Curious, I opened the second of the three paperbacks, *A Purple Place for Dying,* and also found Muff's handwriting there. "I hereby curse the vile Reginald Dinkler for constantly peeing on my shrubs. When this curse is activated, he shall die a truly horrible death. My vengeance extends beyond the grave! Sincerely yours, Eldon Muff."

I looked at the shelf filled with dozens more paperbacks. I

guess the hairy old recluse needed some way to spend his time. I wondered if all the books contained a similar curse.

Before I could check them out, however, a thin and dusty mummy shuffled up to the rack of books, studying them with his extended fingers. His bandages were yellowish brown except for a few swaddles of fresh white gauze where he had patched himself up. His entire head was covered, including his eyes, leaving him blind. He ran his gnarled fingertips along the spines of the paperbacks. "Wonderful. Ah, just wonderful!" he muttered, his voice dry and dusty. "They're in perfect condition." He drew in a long breath. "Mint."

I stepped closer. "I don't have a mint, but I have gum," I offered, quickly realizing that the old mummy needed it.

"No, I mean these books. They're pristine and highly collectible. I want the complete set."

"I already bought three of them," I said, holding up the ones I had taken. "And how can you read? You don't have eyes."

"I don't need eyes to appreciate fine collectibles," the mummy said. "Don't you know who I am?"

"Actually, I don't," I said, and extended my hand. "I'm Dan Chambeaux, zombie private investigator. I'd give you one of my cards, but it wouldn't do you much good."

"I'll remember," said the mummy. "I am Ro-Tar, known since the time of ancient Egypt."

"Most mummies I know come from ancient Egypt," I said, although I had met a few Inca and Aztec mummies. "Normally, the mummification job is a little better. Did they make a mistake preserving your eyes?"

Ro-Tar seemed ashamed. He bent his bandaged head. "Yes, and dozens suffered the same fate. Caused by an improperly trained embalming employee. There was a class action suit." He turned his bandaged, eyeless face toward me. "But my legacy remains. I created a very popular luncheon club for business networking and guest speakers. It was named after me, and it still endures."

"Oh, yes. I've heard of the Rotarians. I didn't know their origin, though."

"Now I'm retired," said the mummy, making me wonder about the retirement age for someone who was thousands of years old. "And I'm an avid collector. I simply must have these paperbacks." He waved his bandaged hand to get Rita's attention. "How much for the books?"

"Two dollars each," the gremlin said without taking a breath. I held on to my three 50¢ paperbacks and didn't point out the price difference.

"Sold! I'll take the lot," Ro-Tar said and cackled in a low voice to me. "She has no idea what these are worth."

Sheyenne called, "Beaux, look what I found!" She lifted several colorful lacy scarves that fell more into the lingerie category than hold-your-hair-against-the-wind category.

Finding my beautiful girlfriend more interesting than old paperbacks, I helped her select several veils that I thought would look best on her. She lifted them with her poltergeist powers, and the wispy fabric drifted around her insubstantial form. I had no idea how or why mangy old Eldon Muff used the sexy scarves, nor did I want to know. What I did care about, though, was how pretty they were going to look on Sheyenne.

Ro-Tar, the blind mummy, was carefully packing his entire collection of pristine paperbacks into his sarcophagus, which had a set of wheels for easier carrying. I tucked my three books under my arm, but frankly my attention was on how Sheyenne would model the colorful scarves later in private.

———

Back at Chambeaux & Deyer Investigations, Sheyenne used her

supernatural skills to organize our office, a task that exceeded the abilities of any mere human.

Robin, my lovely and talented lawyer partner, was busy in her own office preparing notes for an upcoming trial. She was defending a shapeless oily blob that left ugly stains wherever it went. The client had been charged with damage to public property, but Robin's defense was that the blob had a right to exhibit free expression and artistic verve. Regardless of this defense, Sheyenne adamantly refused to let the greasy blob creature into our offices because of the possible damage to our carpets.

The office phone rang before I had a chance to slump into my office chair, where I planned to stare at the folders of unsolved cases. I often expected clues to jump out at me like a cat from a dark alley in a bad horror movie. When I heard McGoo on the line, I realized I should have bought some junk from the estate sale to give him as a thoughtful birthday gift.

"Hey, Shamble—want to see a particularly nasty crime scene? I mean really gross and unbelievable? The victim must have had the worst karma of any person on Earth, off the charts bloody and tragic." He was trying to make it sound like a selling point.

"I'll be right there. You need my help solving it?"

"Not much of a mystery, but this is one for the record books."

I met him at the crime scene just outside of the opera house. The Unnatural Quarter wasn't known for extravagant cultural events, but the Phantom did reasonably well at the opera, especially with his Saturday afternoon children's matinees and with his midnight laser light shows, all accompanied by pipe organ music.

Crime-scene techs had placed yellow tape around a splattered bloody mess that looked like a meat delivery truck had crashed into a shipment of plumbing supplies. Gore and polished pipes were scattered around amongst ivory keys that looked like long rectangular teeth.

I looked up and saw a snapped rope dangling from the pulley near the roof of the opera house, and I realized that these weren't plumbing supplies, but polished pieces of one of the Phantom's grand pipe organs. A bent kid's bicycle lay crashed in the gutter.

Being a detective, even a zombie detective, I didn't need a calculator to put two and two together. The rope hoisting the large pipe organ up to the rooftop level of the opera house had broken, and the huge organ had toppled onto some poor victim on the street. The pipes had fallen straight down and punched through the body like an automated press that mass-produced hamburger patties. Goblin evidence technicians kept busy sorting the mess into tubular debris and mangled-flesh debris, often using tweezers.

"You weren't kidding, McGoo. This is pretty gross."

In front of the building, the Phantom strutted about in his tuxedo, looking distraught. He pulled off the white porcelain mask that covered half of his face, wiped sweat from his ugly visage, and popped the mask back into place. "That was one of my best organs, too."

"It made quite a crash when all those pipes clanged and clattered onto the sidewalk," McGoo said. "Nobody even heard the poor kid scream, although half of the neighbors are now deaf."

"Being deaf might help them enjoy the opera better," I said.

McGoo nodded, as if he hadn't considered that before. He's a redheaded beat cop with a round freckle-spattered face and a grin full of humor that often gets him in trouble. He'd been transferred from a normal precinct to work in the Unnatural Quarter because of his unfortunate penchant for telling politically incorrect jokes.

As he paced around the crime scene tape, looking at the wreckage, the Phantom frowned with the unmasked half of his face. "If the pipes aren't too dented, maybe we can reassemble the whole thing. I don't know about the sound quality, but we could advertise that it's a blood-cursed organ. Imagine the tickets we'd sell."

I looked up at the snapped rope high above. "Why were you hoisting the organ up to the rooftop level?"

"Special springtime event," he said. "We were going to have an open-air barbecue. Hamburgers and hot dogs along with opera. We thought it might catch the lowbrow audience."

"Free hot dogs," McGoo said. "That might even get me listening to opera."

Something still didn't seem right to me about this crime scene. It was too improbable. I saw a couple of burly blue-collar golems standing next to the other end of the broken rope, looking confused because they obviously hadn't finished their job. They had been standing here, using brute force to pull the rope and raise the organ from the sidewalk up to the roof.

"So where did the organ come from in the first place? You were moving it from where to where?"

"It started out in the second-floor gallery," the Phantom said. "We brought it down here and out onto the sidewalk, so the golems could lift it up to the roof."

"And how did it get onto the sidewalk in the first place?"

The Phantom turned to me as if wondering why I was so interested in the mechanics of furniture moving. "The golems carried it out of the second-floor gallery down the stairs onto the street, where they tied the ropes and began hauling it up to the third story, where we could swing it into the attic and then carry it up to the roof."

"But if it was already in the second-floor gallery, why didn't they just carry it up the third flight of stairs?"

The Phantom shrugged, turned to the golems. "Union rules, I think."

I looked at the mangled mess of what had been some poor

unlucky kid on a bicycle. "I guess he was just in the wrong place at the wrong time."

The Phantom clucked his tongue. "He shouldn't have been here at all. I don't even subscribe to his newspaper, and I've tried again and again to stop the kid from throwing papers in front of my opera house. Somebody has to pick them up, and nobody reads them."

"A paperboy?" I asked, suddenly alert.

McGoo said, "Yeah, I guess his name was Bobby Neumann, a zombie kid." He shook his head. "Black and white and red all over, that's for sure."

Bobby Neumann...I knew that name. I suddenly realized it was the same zombie paperboy who had found Eldon Muff dead in his home buried under a pile of monster Hummel figurines. "That's quite a coincidence."

McGoo raised his eyebrows. "You subscribed to the same paper, Shamble?"

"No, not that." I started to explain about the estate sale, but before I got to the part about the curse written inside the old paperback, McGoo received a call on his police radio.

"1063A just occurred at the Gardening and Cemetery Supply Center. It's a 1616 with a 793C."

Around the mess in front of the Phantom's opera house the crime techs also picked up their phones, studied the information, and got ready to move.

McGoo clicked his radio, and his face looked as gray as mine normally did. "Oh, no. Is it a 71B or a 71C?"

The dispatcher hesitated. "71C, I'm afraid."

He groaned. "Oh, this is bad."

Even though I had spent a few years at the police academy before deciding to get my private investigator's license, I hadn't kept up on all the new crime-scene codes. Even so, I felt an odd dread build in my stomach. "I missed some of that, McGoo. What happened, exactly?"

"An awful accident at the home and garden center," he said. "A salesman was demonstrating different models of lawnmowers used to trim cemetery plots. Some teenage werewolf kid had just gotten a job at Greenlawn Cemetery and was there admiring the equipment." He swallowed hard. "But a drunk poltergeist somehow got lost inside the engine of the lawnmower that was being demonstrated, and the demon-possessed gardening machine went berserk. It mowed right over the poor werewolf kid." He shook his head. "Unfortunately, the blades were set to golf-course level, so it trimmed the victim's fur all the way down to his internal organs."

I was amazed that McGoo could have gotten so many details from the code numbers in the police call. "Another truly horrible death. What was the victim's name? The werewolf boy?"

"He was eighteen, so not really a boy, like Bobby Neumann." McGoo glanced over at the mangled pipe organ and the bloody mess on the sidewalk. He asked the dispatcher, who responded, "His name was Reginald Dinkler."

Seeing my shocked look, McGoo said, "Did you know him?"

"I read his name in a book. And Bobby Neumann, too." I narrowed my eyes, settled my fedora more firmly on my head, because I was going to have to do a lot of thinking as a zombie PI. "These aren't just accidents. We've got a curse on our hands."

———

Back in the office, feeling the urgency, I went straight to my desk and picked up the three old paperbacks I'd purchased from the estate sale. I spread them out on the conference room table while McGoo, Robin, and Sheyenne gathered, curious. "Eldon Muff was a thoroughly unpleasant man," I said, "but now I have proof that he was actively evil."

"That old werewolf hated everyone," Robin said. "It's been documented."

"Yes, and he particularly hated the paperboy and the teenage werewolf who peed on his shrubs. He wrote a curse in these two paperbacks." I picked up *Nightmare in Pink* and read Eldon's scrawled writing. "I hereby curse the paperboy Bobby Neumann for his incessant harassment. When this curse is activated, he shall die a truly horrible death. My vengeance extends beyond the grave! Sincerely yours, Eldon Muff."

"Well that does sound suspicious," said McGoo. He had followed me from the crime scene, not understanding what some used paperbacks had to do with horrifically mangled accident victims, although he did admit how much he enjoyed John D. MacDonald's detective novels.

"Being killed by a plummeting pipe organ counts as a horrible death," Sheyenne said.

"And here's the second one." I read aloud the curse from *A Purple Place for Dying*, which identified Reginald Dinkler as the lucky recipient.

I rested my gray-skinned hand on the third book, *Free Fall in Crimson*, holding it closed. "I haven't looked in this one yet."

"But Eldon died some time ago," Sheyenne said. "Why did the curses activate now? This afternoon?"

"I think I triggered them by opening the books and reading the words."

Robin frowned at the old paperbacks. Her brown-eyed stare was intense, and I could see the legal wheels turning in her mind. She had given up a chance at a far more lucrative corporate law practice to see that unnaturals got justice after the Big Uneasy.

McGoo snorted. "Are you suggesting that you're responsible? That the paperboy and the werewolf urinator are dead because you wanted to do a little recreational reading? Whew, I'm glad I don't read much."

"Stranger things have happened," I said.

McGoo scratched his head. "Not many that I can think of." I could probably come up with a few after all my cases, but I didn't want to encourage what would certainly be a lengthy and pointless discussion.

I picked up *Free Fall in Crimson*. "There's one way to find out. If Eldon wrote another curse inside this book, we'll know the target. He always names his victims." I looked at McGoo. "Once the curse is activated, we should have a little time. Do you think you could rally the UQPD fast enough to put protection around the target, whoever or whatever it is?"

McGoo straightened his blue cap on his head. "If we start the paperwork now."

Sheyenne looked nervous. "What if this causes another murder, Beaux?"

"Another *accident*," Robin corrected. "Legally speaking, Dan can't be held responsible since he didn't place the curse. It's clearly not his handwriting."

"I don't want to cause another grisly death," I said, tapping the paperback. "But the curse exists, and it could be triggered anytime the book is opened."

"We could just burn the book," McGoo suggested. "Wouldn't that cancel the curse?"

"I don't like the precedent of book burning," Robin said.

Sheyenne and I both reacted with alarm. I said, "I don't want to mess with curses. There could be nasty unintended consequences, and the horror could spread. If we activate the curse under our own terms, though, at least this way we can respond and try to help the poor victim."

I looked at Robin, then at Sheyenne. Both of them showed

their support. McGoo sighed and took out his police radio. "I'll call it in as soon as we know, just to make sure."

Since I'd just had a fresh embalming treatment last week, my fingers were more nimble than usual. I opened the cover of *Free Fall in Crimson*, turned to the title page, and spotted Eldon's angry handwriting. Bracing myself, I read aloud, "I hereby curse Nolan Pratt for his incompetence as a house painter. He left thin spots on my eastern wall, didn't clean up his mess, overcharged me, and never cleaned out the gutters as he promised. When this curse is activated, he shall die a truly horrible death. My vengeance extends beyond the grave! Sincerely yours, Eldon Muff."

I lurched to my feet, and I'm very good at lurching. "We've got to find this Nolan Pratt and keep him safe."

McGoo was already calling in the report over his police radio. "Send a protective detail right away!" When the dispatcher asked for details, he replied, "We don't know what's going to happen. It's a curse! A meteor could fall from the sky for all I know. Just find Pratt and keep him safe. We're on our way."

We all rushed out of the office together.

———

The curse-prevention response was a military-style operation, like a sophisticated army sweeping in to conquer a small country. The headquarters of Pratt House Painting & Bell Maintenance was just a little office in a business park with one receptionist who had no idea what was happening. She was a fluttery ghost of an old woman who nearly disassociated from fright when she saw the invasion.

"We're a protective detail," McGoo announced as he and I rushed in, accompanied by Sheyenne, Robin, and half of the

UQPD. Everyone was armed to the teeth, and many of them were unnaturals with extravagant teeth, too.

The old receptionist nearly faded away. "But Nolan's not here. He's out on a job."

"Where is he? We need the address," I said. "His life's in danger."

"He's cursed," Robin said, as if it were a legal term.

The receptionist was so flustered she lost control of her poltergeist powers. Fortunately, as a ghost, she didn't need to worry about losing control of her bladder, which she might well have done, considering the panicked expression on her face. The woman fumbled with her intangible hands, but couldn't manage to touch the pages in the appointment calendar. Finally, Sheyenne flitted in and helped her find the location of the painter's current day job.

Armed with the address, our curse-protective detail left the business office and moved our invasion elsewhere, hoping to get to the unsuspecting victim in time.

Nolan Pratt was a broad-shouldered hunchback with shaggy hair, a paint-spattered baseball cap and paint-spattered overalls. He had been contracted to paint a two-story residence with a small but nice front yard, in which he had posted a small sign that said "Painting Courtesy of Pratt House Painting & Bell Maintenance."

Instead of using a ladder, Nolan preferred to dangle from the roof on ropes, swinging about as if he were high up in a belfry somewhere. He hung suspended on the rope harness holding a bucket of paint in one hand and a wide brush in the other. He swung back and forth in pendular arcs, slathering strokes of paint across the house's siding, covering areas in curves rather than straight lines. He missed quite a few spots.

As the fleet of squad cars pulled up to the house with their lights flashing and sirens wailing, the hunchback spilled the bucket of paint down the siding, which actually provided better coverage than his brush had done. He dangled in panic, trapped in the rope harness. McGoo and I led the swarm of the protective detail in a mad dash to rescue the victim, although in his panic Nolan lost his footing and nearly hung himself.

The UQPD came in heavily armed, some with revolvers, some with sniper rifles, others with batons or tear-gas cannisters. McGoo and I drew our respective pistols ready to shoot anything on sight. "We're here to keep you safe," I said.

"House painting isn't really that dangerous," the hunchback replied.

"Get down from there, sir," McGoo said. "Now! For your own protection."

Terrified into cooperating, Nolan extricated himself from the harness and ropes, then sprang to the ground, bouncing on bent legs. "What's all this about?"

"You're cursed," I said. "Eldon Muff wants you to meet with a horrible death—and soon."

"We all wanted that hairy old fart to meet a horrible death." The hunchback snorted. "All my other clients are satisfied. Just look at my rating with the Better Business Bureau."

"This is one of those rare cases where customer satisfaction doesn't count," I said. "Eldon died and left a curse, with you as a specific target. Two other victims have already suffered horrible deaths, a persistent paperboy and a shrub urinator."

The hunchback's expression pinched into one of distaste. "I thought I smelled something in those shrubs." I was surprised he could smell anything, since he reeked of turpentine and sweat.

As I started to describe the curse, a whistling sound came from high above. We all looked up to see a glittering object plummeting straight toward us, straight toward the house, no doubt straight toward the hunchback painter.

"Look out!" I yelled. "Everybody out of the way!"

Even though it sounded ridiculous, McGoo had, in fact, mentioned the possibility of a meteor falling from the sky. Either forgetting or not understanding the concept of protecting someone, the protective detail bolted like cockroaches exposed to the light.

I tackled the hunchback, knocking him into the middle of the lawn an instant before a tumbling blue-white object crashed into the freshly painted side of the house, exactly where Nolan Pratt had been dangling only moments before. The irregular hunk of blue ice broke in shards studded with smeared swatches of paper and frozen oblong brown lumps.

The terrified hunchback picked himself up and stared in astonishment. Sheyenne's ghost swooped close to make sure I was all right. I climbed back to my feet, brushed off my sport jacket, and adjusted my fedora. McGoo and the protective detail came running back, now that it was safe.

Robin stepped up to the broken frozen debris, which had left a crater in the front yard. She looked at it analytically. "Is it a meteor? A comet?"

"Something worse," I said. I had heard about these hazards before, but had never seen one with my own eyes. "It's a frozen ball dumped from an airplane toilet reservoir, a block of ice from the sky. They usually don't make it to the ground, but I guess this was a bigger lump than usual."

"I could've been killed!" Nolan cried.

"And in a most unsanitary way," I said.

Sheyenne drifted close, wrapping her intangible arms around me. "That was close!"

"Is it over now?" McGoo asked. "Did we break the curse?"

"We need to have the curses studied by an expert," Robin said, "but from my preliminary analysis in the legal library, those handwritten curses are inexpensive, one-time-only curses."

"Eldon Muff was very frugal," McGoo agreed.

The hunchback adjusted his paint-spattered baseball cap and looked at the ruined side of the house, not to mention the crater and the blue toilet ice in the front yard. "The customer isn't going to be happy about that, but they signed a specific waiver absolving me of responsibility for meteor strikes."

Robin's brow furrowed. "They might have legal grounds to contest it, sir. A frozen ball of ice and turds from an airplane isn't technically a meteor." When the hunchback looked distraught, she reassured him, "If it comes to that, I'll take the case as your defense attorney."

I felt relieved to see the house painter safe and sound, frazzled but unsoiled by the fecal comet. "We couldn't save Bobby and Reginald from their horrible deaths, but at least we saved Mr. Pratt. And those were the only three curses." I decided never to open the MacDonald paperbacks again.

Then I froze, remembering that the blind mummy had bought dozens more at the estate sale, and I had no doubt that each one of those books held a similar curse.

———

Leaving the UQPD army to clean up the unfortunate residence and lock down the crime scene, McGoo and I commandeered one of the squad cars and raced off to Ro-Tar's house. Robin and Sheyenne joined us, while the rest of the protective detail remained on call, eager for overtime should we need them.

We recognized the mummy's quaint, well-maintained abode by the large Rotarian sign in the front yard. Racing from the parked squad car, we pounded on the front door, urgently yelled the mummy's name, and soon we heard the shuffle-slide of his wrapped footsteps as he came to answer the knock.

When he opened the door, Ro-Tar had fresh bandages wrapped around his eyes like a blindfold. He also wore a stylish paisley smoking jacket, and I was very afraid of what might happen if a burning cigarette touched his flammable bandages. On the bright side, the gauze over his mouth would have filtered the smoke, thereby reducing the carcinogenic hazard.

I blurted out, "We're here about all those collectible paperbacks you bought at the estate sale. They're cursed!"

"We have to confiscate them," McGoo said. "They're already responsible for two deaths and one ruined house painting job."

The blind mummy recognized my voice. "The books are collector's editions, Mr. Chambeaux, and they're not for sale. They are extremely valuable."

"But you don't understand," Sheyenne said. "People are going to die."

The mummy sniffed through empty nasal sockets. "They are murder mysteries, after all."

He politely led us inside his home, which was like a museum. The furniture was distinctly art deco. Framed prints and old movie posters hung on the walls, and shelves and curio cabinets covered the rest of the space. Every inch was crammed with collectibles, eccentric memorabilia from old radio programs, promotional items from long-cancelled TV shows, framed original comic panels. His best items, including the set of classic paperbacks, were stored in magnificent cherry wood bookshelves fronted with locked glass cabinet doors, as if he feared the books might take wing and escape.

"I just displayed all those fine John D. MacDonald paperbacks. Here's the entire collection." Ro-Tar stood in front of the glass-enclosed bookcase, though he couldn't see the contents. "They are absolutely pristine."

"But you can't read them," Robin said. "You have no eyes."

"I have eye sockets. And I can appreciate fine rare books."

I looked at all the spines lined up inside the case, nearly fifty of them. Each paperback had been lovingly sealed in a separate protective plastic bag, then arranged in order behind the transparent cabinet doors.

"We think that each one of those books contains a terrible curse," McGoo said. "If you open them, people will die horrible deaths."

"*Open* them?" Ro-Tar said, recoiling in a different sort of horror. "I wouldn't even touch them! They're protected and preserved, sealed away on display."

"But if you ever read them, you will activate the curse," Robin said.

"Read them!" the mummy scoffed. "They're collector's books! They're not meant to be read, merely to be owned, merely to be coveted." He was growing vehement. "And I will not let you have them. They're perfectly safe with me."

"But if someone—" I began.

"I can assure you, they will never be read, Mr. Chambeaux," Ro-Tar replied. "They'll never be touched. I'll allow no fingerprints on the covers. The spines will never be cracked."

"Then we don't have to worry about the curse being triggered," I said, but I remained curious. "If you don't ever intend to read them, why are you so fascinated with the books?"

"Because I *have* them," Ro-Tar said so vehemently that he coughed dust out of his mouth bandages. "And for a collector, that's the most important thing."

McGoo remained indignant. "Those items are extremely dangerous. We have to take them back to the police station, store them safely in the evidence room."

I had seen the chaos of the UQPD evidence room. More than once, spell-contaminated items had gone missing, sacred amulets had been misfiled, immortality elixirs spilled in birth-certificate files. In contrast, I looked around at the mummy's absolutely pristine and well-maintained collection, the plastic seals on the cursed books, the locked cabinet.

"On second thought, McGoo, these cursed books might be in better hands if they just stay locked up here."

"They will never be in any hands at all," Ro-Tar said. "No one will ever touch them!"

"Exactly what I mean," I said. "We'll know where they are, but the deadly curses will remain sealed. Forever."

"Nothing is forever," Ro-Tar said philosophically, as if it were something he had once heard from a Rotarian luncheon speaker. "But I've been around for thousands of years, and I know how to take care of valuable old things."

Though she remained concerned, Robin came to the same conclusion I had. After considering all the paperwork required to file and maintain each one of these cursed books, signing them into evidence, and then keeping them completely secure, without mishap, McGoo agreed with my assessment. "Sounds like the best curse-prevention we can manage."

Pleased to have visitors, now that we could breathe a sigh of relief about the looming curses, Ro-Tar took the time to show us around his fascinating collection. I became more and more convinced this was a more stable and protected place than the UQPD evidence room. Maybe I could convince McGoo to transfer a few other dangerous artifacts....

When we were ready to go, I said to Sheyenne, "Maybe we'd better avoid estate sales from now on."

"Never again," my ghost girlfriend agreed. "But you don't want me to return all those veils and lingerie, do you?"

"Not just yet," I said. I was looking forward to seeing her model them for me. "They may be collector's items."

NANOTURDS

RAY VUKCEVICH

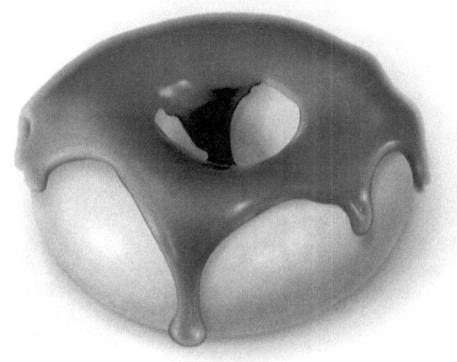

Ray Vukcevich writes a lot of disturbing and cautionary tales, many of which I always remember from the very first time I read the story even if it was twenty-five years ago. This is one of those stories. Hard to forget a guy waking up as a giant, chocolate-coated donut.

As I said last issue, Ray's mind doesn't see story or fiction like any other writer and his stories right from the start have always fit Pulphouse. *I am honored to bring another of his classic stories forward in time for a brand new set of readers. And considering the work going on with nanotechnology right now, maybe giant, chocolate-coated donuts are not far behind.*

———

Dr. Garrett Whistler woke up to find himself transformed into a giant chocolate-coated donut. He rolled out of bed and waddled on stubby legs to the full-length mirror on his closet door. The mirror wasn't wide enough to display his entire girth at once, so he shifted from side to side assessing his new state. His arms were short, stiff, apparently without elbows or wrists, and poked straight out to either side of his donut body. He could move them up and down as if he were trying to fly or flag down a car, but he couldn't have scratched his nose even if he had a nose to scratch. Maybe his best feature, he thought, was a pair of strikingly beautiful sapphire blue eyes set above the big hole that passed through his body. The lashes were long and black, and he found he could bat them seductively.

"Bob!" he yelled and thereby discovered his mouth, a foot-long slit inside and at the bottom of his hole. His pink tongue, as fat as the business end of a garden spade, lolled out onto the floor in front of little legs.

The balance of power must have shifted among his nanopeople, Garrett thought, probably triggered by the reprogramming he had attempted the night before. Clearly, he'd pissed someone off. He needed to get in touch with Bob, his interface, right away.

"Your wish is my command and all that." Bob appeared in his mind's eye.

The translator was, in truth, a network of nanopeople working in shifts, but the picture Garrett saw was of a fatherly little man in a rumpled gray suit and thick glasses. The nanopeople, invisible, sentient, self-replicating robots of nanotechnology, communicated by smell and temperature, and finding the proper neurons in Garrett's brain to fire for sight and sound had been tricky. It had taken them an enormous amount of time (somewhat more than an hour big people time) to establish the interface with Garrett who was their world. Their problem was that Garrett's mind was so much slower than their own minds. A nanoperson could put in a whole day's work between one of Garrett's syllables and the next. They used what was already in Garrett's mind, but he could never predict how they would put the sights and sounds together. It made the translator seem a little moody at times, but at least all the nanopeople who comprised Bob were on Garrett's side — they were all members of GAWHIF (GArrett WHIstler First). Preserving, protecting, and nurturing their world was the guiding philosophy of GAWHIF.

"I see you've noticed the change," Bob said.

Garrett pulled his tongue back into his mouth and said, "Do something!"

Cindy would be here soon so he could drive her to the lab. He couldn't let her see him like this. She'd surely guess he'd said to hell with the rules and introduced a colony of nanopeople into his own body. Although they'd had a brief thing, Dr. Cindy Brown was once again only a colleague, and while she probably had a soft spot or two left for him, she'd still turn him in.

Maybe he could wear a hat and sunglasses.

The colonies were supposed to be locked up tight. There were no plans to move them into big people for years. Garrett hadn't gone along with that. If backed against a wall, he would have argued vehemently that there was no place for secrecy in science, that sometimes big chances had to be taken for big gains. He was more honest with himself. Nanotechnology promised long life and good health. It promised enhanced mental powers. Garrett feared that he would be like the last person executed before the death penalty was abolished forever, that the nanopeople would be available just a little too late for him, that he would die before the dawn of a bright new age of immortality.

"We are trying," Bob said.

"What about the reinforcements I injected last night?"

Sometime after breakfast the day before, Bob had reported that BIFOP (the Body Is FOr People!) had dotted Garrett's cells with donut shops, cookie stands, and pizza parlors. All the spilled coffee had set Garrett's nerves on edge, and he'd left the lab early, leaving Cindy to find another ride home. He'd picked up some fast food without getting out of his car, and by the time he got home, Bob reported that the first hamburger place had been established near Garrett's liver. It took only milliseconds to clog the area with NanoBurger boxes. Before turning in for the night he'd programmed and injected a troop of zealous repro-grammers dedicated to garbage recycling. Apparently they had wimped out on him.

"I told you that was not a good idea," Bob said. "Sentient means not easily programmed. I did warn you. BIFOP crushed or converted your so-called reinforcements in a matter of your minutes."

The scene washed away and was replaced by a holiday parade — cotton candy floats, lines of kazoo players, high school marching bands, and, ominously, a company of goose-stepping soldiers all grim-faced and heavily armed. Spectators lined the litter-choked streets, cheering and whistling and jerking signs up and down: One World Is Not Enough! What's In It For Us? Replication Is A Divine Duty!

"I'm afraid you may have to do what they want," Bob said, sounding sad and defeated.

"I can't do that," Garrett said.

From behind, scabbed and clawed hands closed around Bob's neck. "Yikes!" he cried as he was snatched from sight. A dark form with glowing red eyes muscled into Garrett's brain, filling his mind with slimy green light, the sound of cats mamboing with radiator fans on winter mornings, the smell of burning hair and sour milk.

"Okay, Dr. Whistler. No more Mr. Nice Guy."

"Who are you?"

From somewhere in the gloom, the thing that crouched like a spider in Garrett's brain chuckled. "You can call me Jimmy."

Garrett shuddered. He couldn't have said why that name disturbed him, but it did. "What do you want?"

The gloom receded and Garrett saw Jimmy lounging back naked on a rumpled motel bed, a starving artist's rendition of some ocean behind his head. He held a greasy cheeseburger in one hand and with the other slowly stroked his pink erection. There was a dead white roll of fat around his middle. His hair was neatly trimmed and combed, and on his face was a look of horrible lust, somehow guilty and delighted at once.

"A world of our own," Jimmy said. "A world without those bleeding heart GAWHIF guys. All you got to do is what comes naturally." He grinned and gave his tool a few good jerks for emphasis, wiggled his eyebrows up and down. "The little lady should be ringing your doorbell about one...two...three...now!"

Nothing happened.

Jimmy scowled.

The doorbell rang.

"Garrett?" Cindy Brown called.

"Show time," Jimmy said.

Panic flooded Garrett, and he flapped his little arms like an irritated chicken. He wouldn't answer the door. He wouldn't leave his bedroom. She'd go away. He backed against the wall and held his breath.

Cindy rang the bell again and shouted his name and then became quiet. Garrett let out his breath in a whoosh as relief washed through him.

Then he heard his front door open. He'd forgotten she still had a key.

"Come on, Garrett," she called. "I don't want to be late."

He heard her heels clicking on the hardwood floor as she walked across his living room. "Garrett, are you sick or what?" She edged his bedroom door open and peeked inside.

From where he'd flattened himself against the wall, he could see her nose and a cascade of blond hair falling over the side of her face. If it had not been for her hair, she would have surely seen him.

"Christ," she said and pushed into the room.

She walked toward his unmade bed, and Garrett felt a sudden rush of lust as he watched her perfect bottom moving beneath her skirt. That moment of weakness was enough for Jimmy, and Garrett felt his mind flood with the sound of angry bees. He was pushed to one side, forced to some place where he could watch but no matter how hard he tried could not control his chocolate-coated body.

Cindy stood with her hands on her hips looking down at his bed. Garrett felt himself sneak up behind her. Just before he reached her, she turned sharply to face him. She put her hands over her ears and screamed. Garrett rushed forward and bumped her, and she fell back on the bed, her legs arching up as she landed.

Garrett felt his knees bend and coil like springs and his body launched itself into the air. His hole slipped over Cindy's legs, and by the time her feet hit the floor, he was lodged around her lower body like an inner tube around a woman on the beach. He felt his donut hole shrink to hold her tight. He looked over her stomach and beyond her heaving breasts to see her lift her head and scream again. He could imagine her horror looking down her body to see his sapphire eyes staring at her. At least he wasn't equipped to do what Jimmy and BIFOP wanted him to do. If she didn't die of fear, Cindy might come through this okay.

But wait! Something moved down there.

He felt a delicious genital tingle as BIFOP transmuted his tongue and used it to probe her underwear. Her eyes grew wide, and she stopped screaming. Then he heard the ripping of fabric and the hot wash of her as he entered and she screamed again. Part of his mind wondered at the angle and admired the engineering BIFOP had accomplished in building his member a flexible snake at the base and a steel hard rod at the tip. He felt electricity zapping through every cell of his body, and he was jerked along with the nanopeople of the BIFOP faction as they rushed to catch the seminal subway cars to a new world. He saw them as he imagined they really were — great riverboats paddling through the seas of his cells, breaking down the cell walls in their headlong rush to catch the train. He felt them being whisked away as he exploded inside Cindy.

Those beings comprising Jimmy held on to the very last moments, and Garrett could feel himself gaining control as they left. The last to go, before rushing away to catch the last drop of transportation had only this to say to him: "We're outta here!"

Cindy's eyes rolled, and she dropped her head back onto the bed. Her arms and legs flopped and jerked in a fit of transformation as the members of BIFOP took up their places in her cells.

Finally, she was still, and then she raised her head to look at him. He saw the realization dawning on her face as BIFOP told her the score. "Garrett, you didn't! How could you be so stupid?"

Then there was no Cindy in her face. Her arms jerked and rippled as if there were trapped animals under her skin struggling to get out. Her biceps bulged like a weight lifter's arms, and she seized him, peeled him off her body, and tossed him to the floor. She sat up on the bed and stretched like a jungle cat waking in a new night. She reached down with those great hands and arms and lifted him off the floor and crushed his hole into a long vertical slit. He felt bones snap and blood flow. She set him on the floor and put one hand above his eyes and flattened him. Then she stood up and kicked him into a corner. He hit the wall with a splat and left a long streak of blood and chocolate as he fell to the floor.

Garrett rolled over and watched her straighten her clothes, and for just a moment he thought he saw Cindy in her eyes as her arms shrank to normal and she wiped her chocolate-smeared hands on her skirt and pushed her tangled blond hair from her face.

"Oh, Garrett, what have you done? What have you done?"

Her body stiffened and she grabbed herself between her legs. "No more than you'll do, Honey Pot," she said in a deep demon voice.

The leer left her face, and she stomped her foot on the floor. "You may have bitten off more than you can chew with me, Buster," she said in her own sweet voice, filled now with determination.

"Oh, yeah?" she answered herself in those awful deep tones. She jerked herself up on her toes, spun around like a marionette, marched to the bedroom door, and was gone. Garrett felt the apartment shake as she slammed the front door.

Garrett groaned. He hurt everywhere. Without the nanopeople to maintain his donut body, he would soon die.

Cindy wouldn't be enough for BIFOP. What had he loosed upon the world? Dying was perhaps no more than he deserved, but he hoped it would happen fast.

He imagined himself drifting over his broken and dry cells — a bombed-out landscape of garbage and waste. On the sands of a dead sea, he saw the rusted hulk of a riverboat — one of the nanopeople who didn't get away. He floated down to its deck and landed like a falling leaf. He stood with his hands on the rail and looked out over the sea bottom dotted here and there with small ponds of cell fluid. He squinted into a glaring sun as the sound of helicopters whomp whomp whomped from somewhere far away.

"Garrett?"

"Bob?"

"Yeah, it's us." Bob's voice filled his head, and he saw maybe a half dozen black dots moving low over the dead sea. The helicopters converged on him quickly, and as their blades cut the sunlight and tossed shadows onto the deck of the riverboat, Garrett grew large and was whisked away through a starry darkness.

He opened his eyes and saw that he was no longer a donut. Instead he seemed to be an infant, pink and uncoordinated, his arms and legs pumping energetically in the air.

"We lost a lot of mass," Bob said. "Had to slough off a lot of dead cells. We'll do what we can. There are so few of us. But at least we're rid of most of those BIFOP turds."

Garrett felt a rush of warmth as his urine arched into the air and splashed upon his stomach.

He explored his toothless gums with his tongue and shivered in his nakedness. He couldn't survive alone.

"What should I do, Bob?" he shouted in his mind.

"You might try crying," Bob said and was gone again.

"It's all right. Drink. There are only a few nanoturds in it."

QUEEN OF THE MOUSE RIDERS

ANNIE REED

I had to fight hard for this original story from Annie Reed when I first saw it a year ago. Not because Annie didn't want to sell it to me, but because other editors wanted it as much as I did. That's how good Annie is.

Her stories have appeared in dozens of magazines and she is considered one of the best short story writers coming into fiction in the last decade. I am proud to say her stories appear regularly in Fiction River *and I hope to have many of them in future issues of this magazine as well.*

Thanks, Annie, for letting the readers of Pulphouse *see this wonderful story first.*

———

Gurgling yowls echoed off the tiled floor in Sarah's bathroom. Bounced off the ceiling, gaining strength, and intruded on what was turning out to be a very, very nice dream featuring the star of a movie she'd watched just before bed.

In the dream, the star turned his incredibly expressive eyes in Sarah's direction, smiled his best enigmatic smile, and said, "Pardon me, darling, but is that your cat?"

(In the dream he'd turned British. She happened to know he'd been born and raised in the Bronx. Dreams were just plain weird sometimes.)

"Yes," she said. "She's apparently caught a mouse."

Starlight the Cat had a battle cry like a two-note yodeler gargling mouthwash. She reserved that particular cry for whenever she caught a mouse. Or something that looked like a mouse. Or a mouse-shaped stuffed toy.

Most of the time she'd only caught one of her toys. Thank goodness. But on at least one memorable occasion she'd interrupted a visit from Sarah's mother by presenting a live mouse as the third course for their lunch date.

Sarah's mother was deathly afraid of mice.

So where did Starlight drop the mouse? Right at her mother's feet, of course.

Sarah's mother had screamed. Starlight had looked suitably insulted at having her contribution to the meal rejected. And the mouse? It had attempted a quick getaway, but Sarah had thrown a kitchen towel over the poor thing, taken it for an elevator ride—where she'd gotten a few odd looks from her neighbors—and released it into the wild in the bushes outside her apartment building.

She'd laid out traps after that, but no more mice appeared, living or dead.

The dream, complete with the suddenly British Bronx-born movie star, dissolved completely as Sarah sat up in bed. She groped for her cell, thumbed it on to read the time—two thirty-eight!—and squinted in the general direction of her bathroom.

The next to last thing in the world she wanted to do was get out of bed, but the very last thing she wanted to do was discover mouse guts in her bed anytime soon. Or feel a live mouse running over her face. Yuck!

The nightlight next to the bathroom sink threw a faint ghostly glow into Sarah's bedroom. She slid out of bed and shivered as her feet hit the cold hardwood of her bedroom floor.

"It's a good thing I love you, kitty cat."

She tucked her feet inside her fuzzy pink slippers and pulled on the zippered hoodie she'd left on the other side of her bed.

She really needed to buy herself a robe one of these days. For late-night mouse rescuing, if nothing else. And there hadn't been anything else in longer than she cared to remember, hence the promising dream.

Starlight did her gargle-yowl again, louder this time.

"Coming, mousie," Sarah said. "And don't you dare eat it, baby girl, you hear me?"

A second sound echoed off the bathroom tiles. Not a squeak—Sarah would have expected that—but an angry shout. A very high-pitched, tiny shout.

Sarah stopped short, blinked, and then pinched herself on the arm to make sure she was awake.

"Ouch!"

Yup. Definitely awake, and probably bruised to boot.

So what in the world was going on in her bathroom?

She crept to the bathroom door, turned the light on, and poked her head inside.

Starlight was crouched in her hunter-kitty pose. She held something in her mouth that was vaguely mouse-shaped with brownish-gray fur and a long, thin tail. Only the tail had a fuzzy puff of fur at its twitching tip.

Mice didn't have fuzzy tails, did they?

And they certainly didn't have something that looked like a tiny saddle on their backs or little bits of colorful string on their heads that looked like a bridle.

Sarah took all that in at a glance. What really caught her attention was the tiny figure standing right in front of Starlight shouting at her cat.

The figure was shaped like a man, but that's where the resemblance ended. No more than three inches tall, it was covered in grayish fur—at least the parts that Sarah could see since it was wearing tiny little pants—and had a sharp snout where a person's nose would be. It had big, mouse-like ears on the sides of its head, a raised row of darker fur that ran from the top of its head down the back of its spine, and held something long and sharp-looking in a hand that really looked like a rodent's paw, only with an opposable thumb. It was shouting at Starlight in a language Sarah couldn't understand.

She'd never seen anything like it. She wasn't even sure anything like this could really exist in the world.

She pinched her wrist this time, which convinced her—yet again—that she really was awake.

Okaaay. Now what?

Practical Sarah took over. Whatever this thing was, it was threatening her cat. Maybe it had something to do with the mouse-thing Starlight had caught.

"Hey, Starlight?" Sarah kept her voice low. "Maybe you should drop the mousie."

The little creature with the weapon turned his head toward her when she spoke, but it was little more than a glance. It (he?) was clearly more concerned with Starlight. She supposed she would be too if she was in its position.

Sarah crouched down next to her cat. "Good kitty." She petted Starlight on her head and then grabbed the cat by the scruff of her neck before she could run away with the mouse.

Or whatever it was.

Starlight's gurgling-yowl changed to an angry growl, but after a moment, she dropped the mouse.

Or whatever it was.

The little thing ran over to the tiny warrior person, and it (he) climbed on the mouse's back.

Sarah expected the mouse and rider to make a beeline for the bathroom door. She jumped to her feet to get out of the way—wherever they came from, they were welcome to go right back there, thank you very much—but she needn't have bothered.

They headed toward her wicker shelves instead.

Sarah hadn't done much in the way of decorating her bathroom, but her one extravagance was a white wicker shelving unit that held her extra towels. It gave her bathroom a little girlish personality—white wicker, rose-colored towels—and looked pretty against the gray tiles on the floor.

The bottom shelf had just enough clearance from the floor for the mouse and its rider to fit.

Oh, wonderful. She'd have to shoo them out from beneath her shelves. Throw one of her towels over them, cart them downstairs, and release them outside. The last time she'd done that she hadn't been wearing a nightshirt, a hoodie, and fuzzy pink slippers. Here's hoping it was too late at night to run into any of her neighbors.

Starlight crouched down in front of the wicker shelves, the fur on her tail poofed out as fat as a feather duster. She was still hunting them. Of course. She was a cat, and that's what cats did.

Sarah scooted Starlight out of the way with one fuzzy slippered foot, earning another growl.

"I'll make this up to you later," she said.

She grabbed a bath towel off the top of the stack on the bottom shelf and unfolded it, took a deep breath to steady her nerves, and moved the unit away from the wall.

But there was nothing there.

Nothing but the tiled floor that had always reminded her of the way clouds looked on a warm spring morning.

"Where did they go?" Sarah asked.

Starlight flicked her tail in annoyance and stalked out of the bathroom. Sarah supposed that was about as good an answer as she'd get.

She got down on her hands and knees to peer underneath the bottom shelf. Not a thing, unless a couple of minor-league dust bunnies counted.

She took all the towels off the shelves and shook them out, one by one, but nothing fell on the floor.

She even felt along the bathroom wall. Other than an uneven spot where there was a seam in the molding, she felt nothing out of the ordinary.

She put her hands on her hips and sighed. What, exactly, did she expect? A secret doorway or something? One of those mouseholes like she saw in the cartoons she watched when she was a kid? A cute little miniature door complete with handle and hinges and tiny flowerpots on either side?

"You're losing it," she muttered.

A huge yawn overtook her. As her jaws creaked, she thought about how silly the whole thing had been. Starlight had caught a mouse, that was all. The rest of it never happened. She'd had a very vivid dream brought on by a great movie, a sexy star (who really should be British), and a total lack of love life.

She slid the wicker shelves back into place, folded and replaced the towels, and turned the light off. Her bed, and hope-fully her dream date, awaited.

Starlight was already curled up on the other side of the bed, pretend sleeping. Only the flicking tip of her tail gave her away.

"Good kitty." Sarah scritched Starlight behind one ear. "Good to know you're here to protect me."

And the mouse?

Sarah didn't have the energy to go looking for it. It would go back to wherever it came from, or she'd deal with it in the morning.

At least with Starlight on the bed, no sane mouse would come anywhere near her.

Famous last words.

––––––––

Sarah had brought Starlight home from the pound after a particu-larly bad breakup.

Not with a guy, but with chocolate.

And coffee.

And black tea.

And salt.

Basically anything that would kick her heart rate into over-drive was off the menu. Permanently.

Tea? Okay, she could give up that. She even learned to live with herbal alternatives, some of which were pretty tasty.

Coffee was harder. Decaf tasted nasty and, as it turned out, wasn't totally caffeine free. Even though her cardiologist gave her the raised eyebrow and the not-quite-as-comforting-as-it-sounded opinion that "it won't kill you," all the poundy, skippy heartbeats made her feel miserable, so out with the decaf, too.

And potato chips. Canned soups. Salted nuts. All out.

Chocolate, though—that had been hard.

Sarah had been a chocoholic all her life. Pretty much anything chocolate topped her list of Best Things To Eat Ever. Chocolate cake, brownies, chocolate chip cookies, homemade fudge. Hot chocolate. Mocha lattes. Even chocolate chips right out of the bag. Total comfort food.

And all strictly verboten.

It took her months to say goodbye to chocolate, and like any emotional breakup, there'd been setbacks. Times when she'd thought just a cookie here or a bit of brownie there wouldn't be so bad. Reality, of course, had taught her otherwise.

The fourth time she quit chocolate cold turkey, she found herself at the pound adopting the cat named Starlight.

Starlight was a beautiful big girl with long white fur and sapphire blue eyes. She had the faintest brownish tabby markings down her spine and around her nose and eyes. She'd been in a room with a bunch of other adult cats, but while those cats played or slept sprawled out on the furniture, Starlight sat on the highest platform of the room's lone cat tree like a regal princess surveying her kingdom.

The volunteer at the pound didn't know much about Starlight's background, only that she'd been surrendered by her former owner because she'd been a "difficult" cat. They could only guess at her age—somewhere in the adult range without being a senior kitty.

Sarah didn't even hesitate at the "difficult" description. The moment she'd looked in Starlight's eyes, she'd felt like the two of them had been meant for each other. If it was possible to be soul-mates with a cat, Sarah had found hers. She took Starlight home, and for the past two years—except for the unfortunate mouse incident during that luncheon with her mother—Starlight had never been even close to difficult.

Until tonight.

Another yowl woke Sarah up from a sound sleep at five minutes to four.

This yowl had nothing to do with hunting and everything to do with feline anger.

Sarah could commiserate.

"Starlight, what in the world?"

This time Sarah didn't need the nightlight from her bathroom to see what was going on. If she could believe her eyes, that was.

Starlight was crouched on the foot of Sarah's bed. The cat was surrounded by at least a half dozen of the weird little mousies and their riders, each of them glowing with a soft, luminous golden light.

Sarah blinked and rubbed her eyes, but when she opened them again, she saw the same thing.

Or almost the same thing.

This time she saw the little man perched like a bird on top of her dresser on the other side of her bed.

"Hey!" She pulled the covers up to her chest, dislodging half the mouse riders from their mounts in the process. "What are you all doing in my apartment!" She pulled the covers up higher. "And in my room!"

She didn't expect an answer—she hadn't understood the mouse rider before, so it stood to reason (reason! ha!) that they couldn't understand her. So she was more than a little surprised when the man on her dresser spoke back.

"We've come to take the dragon home," he said.

He was maybe all of two feet tall—hard to tell the way he was crouched down with his arms wrapped around his knees—with dark brown hair that brushed his shoulders and a vaguely mousey-looking face. Sharp nose, receding chin, but not at all hairy.

And he spoke with a British accent.

Of course.

Didn't it mean you were going nuts when your hallucinations spoke to you in the same voice as the cute actor in your dreams?

And did he say dragon?

"What dragon?" she asked.

The little man nodded at Starlight. "They've been seeking her for some time now. Ever since she..." He paused, looking for all the world like a man who's lost his train of thought. It didn't take long before he snapped back. "'Went on walkabout,' I believe is the phrase you use on this side."

Not British. Australian. Easy to confuse the two when you're losing your mind at four in the morning.

"This side of what?" she asked, refusing to deal—for the moment—with the fact that this strange little man (who was in her apartment!) thought her cat was a dragon.

"The divide," he said, as if that explained everything.

"The divide."

"I can understand the appeal. I've been here myself for three moons now. Great food. Especially—what's it called? Chocolate? Marvelous stuff."

Of course. Her diminutive nighttime invader was a choco-holic. Could this get any weirder?

Maybe she shouldn't ask.

"You do realize that's my cat, not a dragon," she said.

The fluffy dragon/cat was currently hissing and spitting at the mouse riders, who didn't seem all that concerned.

Why wasn't she swatting them? Starlight had a pretty good right hook, something Sarah had discovered when she'd lobbed a scrunched-up CD wrapper at Starlight just to see what she'd do. Starlight had punched the thing right out of the air.

Maybe it was the weird glowing faerie lights.

Faerie lights. Had she just really thought that?

The little man shrugged. "Cat. Dragon. What's the difference?"

Dragon—big scaly beast who breathes fire.

Cat—cute, cuddly predator who catches mice and purrs when you scritch her under the chin.

Not the same thing.

"Cats don't breathe fire," she said.

His eyebrows raised, giving his strange, mouse-like face a cartoonish look of surprise. "Your dragons breathe fire?"

She sighed. "We don't have dragons, but if we did, they'd breathe fire."

"That doesn't make any sense."

"I know *exactly* what you mean."

Starlight screeched as one of the mouse riders, still surrounded by that golden glow, took several small steps toward her.

"Hey!" Sarah yanked at the covers. "You leave my cat alone!" But this time the mouse riders were ready for her. They stood their ground.

This was ridiculous.

"I don't know who you think you are, but you better leave her alone."

She didn't want to hurt anyone, but she wasn't going to let them hurt Starlight, who clearly didn't want anything to do with any of this weirdness.

Sarah leaned over, intending to brush the little mousies and their riders off the bed.

When her hand touched the golden light surrounding one of the riders, the room seemed to suddenly *shift*. Not so much in location—it was still her room, and she was still sitting on her bed—but instead of a cold, dark, kind of utilitarian rented apartment, she got an impression of warmth and growing things and little specks of light that were really tiny beings who lived in the air.

"Whoa," Sarah said, pulling her hand back. She rubbed it where it stung from the contact with the faerie light.

No wonder Starlight didn't want to touch them.

"They're not going to hurt her, but they're not going to let her go, either," the little man on her dresser said. "She's their queen."

Queen?

Her cat was the Queen of the mouse riders.

Could this night *get* any weirder?

"Well then, can you tell them to stop doing that to her?" Sarah waved her still-stinging hand at the mouse riders. "She doesn't like it."

Starlight was crouched down on the bed, her beautiful blue eyes dilated nearly black. She'd never looked less like the regal princess she had in the pound, and that nearly broke Sarah's heart.

"And you can't take her away," she said again. "She's my only real friend."

Which was actually true. Sure, she had work acquaintances, and there was her mother. Now that Sarah had grown up and moved out of her mother's house, they actually had a pretty good relationship. But the only one who really shared her life—her ups and downs and all the secrets she could never tell another living soul—was Starlight.

"Well, of course you can come with her," the little man said. "You're the servant to the dragon."

Servant to the dragon?

"I am *not*—" she started to say, but then she thought about who cleaned the litter box and who bought the food and who stopped doing whatever it was she was doing whenever Starlight wanted to sit on her lap or be petted. Sarah couldn't remember the last time she'd opened a book without Starlight draping herself over the exact page Sarah was trying to read.

Maybe she *was* the dragon's servant.

"What if I don't want to go either?" she asked. "And go where, exactly? And how did you get here anyway?"

"Through the door," he said.

She wasn't sure if that was an answer to the second or third question. But either way, it didn't make any sense.

"You couldn't have come in through the door. I'd have heard you. It's locked and I set the alarm."

He scratched his head and looked at her with one eyebrow raised. "You know how to lock a door?" He shifted on the dresser and stretched out one leg, grunting with the effort. "I don't even know how to do that, and I'm sure you didn't know it was there. Not many people on this side do."

As he spoke, she realized his Aussie accent had totally disappeared. Now he sounded like he'd lived in her neighborhood all his life.

Not that it mattered. He was clearly nuts because *she* was clearly nuts, and in the land of the crazy, accents came and went. Just like her dream British version of that actor from the Bronx.

Starlight's yowl turned into an angry shriek.

Sarah realized she'd only really been paying attention to the little man on her dresser. She whipped her head around toward her cat, who'd been backed into a proverbial corner...er, circle.

The little mouse riders had all converged on Starlight. Their golden light formed a nearly solid ring with Starlight in the center, and she'd clearly had enough. Her ears were back, her teeth were bared, and if she could have breathed fire, Sarah's bed would be in flames.

Starlight was going to fight back, and when she did—when she touched that ring of golden light—well, Sarah had a sick feeling that's how the mouse riders would retake their queen.

And here she'd been, sitting on her bed the whole time, doing nothing but talking to the little man about doors that didn't exist.

He'd been intentionally distracting her.

And she'd let him.

"You bastard," she said.

She dove for Starlight, and the mouse riders closed the last little gap in the ring of light.

Sarah grabbed Starlight, but she was too late.

The foot of her bed disappeared.

All of them—the mouse riders and their mounts, Sarah and her yowling cat—plunged through the portal in the center of that ring of light.

———

The first thing Sarah felt was a soft bapping against her cheek. Fuzzy and rough, with just a hint of pinpricks.

"Wake up," came a soft, scratchy voice. "You've been asleep long enough, my dear."

Sarah managed to slit one eye open. Sort of. Her brain felt mushy and someone had stuffed her head full of cotton. Her nose tickled all the way up to her eyebrows, and a headache hung just on the horizon of wakefulness. Her chest felt heavy like she might be coming down with a cold.

Boy, she must have had way too much wine last night with that movie. Or...did she have any wine at all? She couldn't remember. But she must have because she certainly had the hangover of all hangovers to go with it.

She closed her eye against the golden first light of morning. She didn't need to be up at the crack of dawn. She had another good hour, at least, before her alarm went off, so why in the world was her mother trying to wake her up?

Only that wasn't quite her mother's voice, was it?

Sarah forced her eyes open and came face to face with Starlight, who was sitting upright on Sarah's chest, one paw raised next to Sarah's cheek.

"That's better," Starlight said.

Sarah blinked and opened her eyes all the way.

Her cat was talking. Her *cat* was talking! Her cat was—

"I've gone totally crazy," she muttered. "Instead of little mouse people"—now that she'd opened her eyes, she remembered that part of last night clearly—"I'm imagining I'm in one of those kids' movies where dogs and cats talk."

She'd always thought the talking-pet movies were kind of creepy. She'd told Starlight so many secrets during the time they'd been together, the mere thought that Starlight could pass that information along was just plain *Wrong* with a capital W.

Starlight bapped Sarah again with her right paw. Sarah felt definite pinpricks this time.

"Ow!"

"I'm sorry, dear," Starlight said. "I realize this is all quite a shock, but you need to snap out of it."

Shock? That put it mildly.

Compared to discovering that her cat could talk, accepting the rest of what her senses told her about where she was should have been a breeze. Especially since she'd gotten a preview when that golden faerie light had stung her hand.

She was laying on a bed. Not her bed, unless her bed was made out of overstuffed pillows decorated with tiny, living flowers in a myriad of colors. She felt a sneeze coming on and stifled it. Teach her not to take her allergy meds before bed, but who knew?

The room she and Starlight were in wasn't exactly a room, but more like a hollow inside a very large tree. Like the largest tree Sarah had ever seen, only with windows cut through the living wood decorated with more grasses and flowers and an arched doorway. A gathering of little floaty sprites or faeries hovered near the top of the hollow, giving the room its soft light.

"Where are we?" Sarah asked.

Starlight sat back on her haunches. "On my side of the divide. Those little hooligans succeeded in opening the portal. I'm sorry you were dragged through along with me."

Divide. Again. "Divide between what?"

Starlight sighed. It was a weird thing to see—a cat sighing in frustration. "Between your world and the world of magic. You didn't think all the magic in creation simply disappeared in the age of enlightenment, did you?"

Sarah hadn't really given it much thought before tonight.

"The two merely separated," Starlight said. "Magic on one side, technology on the other."

"But not all the way."

"No. Although so far, only the magic side has been able to open a portal. Intentionally."

Those sapphire blue eyes were staring intently at her again. "Did I do something to open a portal?" Sarah asked. "To put you in jeopardy?"

Another kitty sigh. "No. I did." Starlight lifted a paw and began to wash her face—a kitty stalling tactic if Sarah ever saw one—but then stopped. "I gifted you a dream."

The British-sounding movie actor was a gift from her *cat?* "You did that?"

Come to think of it, Starlight sounded vaguely British too. Dowager British. Maybe she really was a queen.

"You've been alone for some time," Starlight said. "I remember how that felt."

Good lord. Even her cat felt sorry for her. Sarah really had to do something about her love life—if she ever got out of here.

Starlight's ears flicked backward, and her tail whipped around her haunches.

"The little annoyances are coming back," she said.

"The mouse riders?"

"The gods' idea of karma for all the mice my kind killed before the split."

"When they made you their queen." The gods in this world apparently had a keen sense of irony. "And the mice people were okay with that?"

Starlight sighed again. "Even here, people want to be ruled by someone powerful enough to protect them."

"Or eat them."

"There is that, my dear," Starlight said, with a positively wicked look on her face.

"But you don't want to be their ruler." That much had been obvious by how hard Starlight had fought to stay on the other side—Sarah's side—of the portal.

"Ruling people who are afraid of you is tedious. I grew tired of finding new ways to torture them."

Cats did play with their prey. That was the whole reason the mouse Starlight had brought to Sarah's mother had still been alive. Starlight hadn't been done playing with it yet.

Still, the idea of Starlight deliberately torturing the mouse riders because she was bored? More than a little disquieting.

"It's a wonder they don't rise up against you," Sarah said.

"I wish they would! Or at least depose me. I find life much more agreeable on your side of the divide. At least with you."

"Awww. That's sweet." Sarah started to reach up to scritch

Starlight behind one ear, then paused. "Is that okay? I mean, is it okay to do that here?"

Starlight purred deep in her throat. "If you don't let the little annoyances catch you. Behavior unbecoming a queen and all that."

Sarah scritched Starlight, starting behind one ear and ending up beneath her cat's chin.

Starlight's purr increased in volume and she got up on all four paws so she could knead Sarah's ribcage. Sarah would probably have little paw-sized bruises all along her ribs later, but she didn't care. Starlight was acting like the cat she'd always loved, and it clearly made Starlight as happy as it made Sarah.

"Why didn't you ever talk on my side?" Sarah asked.

"Mmmm, right there," Starlight said, sticking her chin out for more rubs. "Would have given me away just as surely as giving you the dream. None of us talk on your side."

None of them? "Are all kitties like you, then? Magic? From this side?"

"Heavens, no. But there are more of us than you think. We're usually labeled 'difficult' and rarely stay on your side for long. Even among cats, we're more independent than most. Otherwise?" Starlight did the kitty equivalent of a shrug—flicking her tail to one shoulder. "No one would be able to tell us apart."

"No one?" Sarah was beginning to get a glimmer of an idea. "Not even on this side?"

Starlight's tail flicked again. "What are you thinking of? I can see in your eyes that something's going on in that head of yours."

Sarah smiled. "I have an idea how to get us both home."

———

Sarah's idea would only work if no one had heard Starlight speak since she'd been on the magic side of the divide. Starlight confirmed that she hadn't spoken to any of the "little annoy-ances" and assured Sarah that the tiny beings of light who hovered at the top of the hollow inside the great tree did not concern themselves with such things.

"Think of them as mosquitoes," Starlight said. "Without the bloodsucking bites."

Finally—something to recommend this side of the divide.

Sarah never thought she'd get tired of flowers, but they were *everywhere* here, and she'd been stifling sneezes ever since she woke up. Her portal-traveling hangover was only marginally better, and her stomach was rumbling. Starlight had offered her something that looked like fresh-mown grass mixed with fermented leaves, which Sarah had politely but firmly declined.

Sarah had explained her plan to Starlight, who'd first looked affronted, but then, as the idea took hold, got that wicked look on her face again.

"Think of it as playacting," Sarah told her. "You want to go home, don't you?"

The plan went into motion when the first of the mouse riders marched into the hollow of the tree. Sarah wasn't surprised to see they were accompanied by the little man who'd perched on her dresser.

"I don't know what you did to me," Sarah said, working up a good head of righteous anger. It wasn't all that hard. "But I want you to send us home!"

The little man shrugged. "You can go home, but the queen must stay."

"She's not a queen, she's a cat! And she's mine!"

Sarah picked up Starlight and held her in a tight hug. Usually that would have earned her an annoyed meow, an angry tail flick, and racing stripes on her arms from Starlight's back claws as she launched herself to the floor.

Instead, Starlight wrapped her front paws around Sarah's neck and issued a pitiful little meow.

"You're scaring her," Sarah said before she began whispering baby-talk nonsense in Starlight's ear.

The little man blinked, then turned to the mouse riders. More had come in the hollow, and even more were crowding around the door, trying to get a look inside. Sarah had lost count of how many there were. Most of them were holding weapons.

The little man chattered at the mouse riders who'd first come in—some sort of a welcoming delegation?—then turned back to Sarah.

"You are mistaken," he said. "They were drawn to her because she performed magic."

"What magic? She's a cat!" Sarah knew what magic they were talking about, but she wasn't about to tell them.

More chattering between the little man and the mouse riders who were now gesturing angrily at Sarah and Starlight.

Sarah felt another sneeze coming on and did her best to stifle it. Unfortunately, pollen won this time and Sarah let out a squeaky "choo!"

The mouse riders immediately stopped chattering at the little man and stared openly at Sarah. A few of the riders around the door scampered away, leaving their weapons behind.

"Don't do that!" The little man looked as scared as the mouse riders he was translating for. "You don't know the power you wield!"

With a sneeze? Who knew?

"Well, I sneeze all the time. I take pills for it, but they're obviously not working here, so you better let us go home before I sneeze again!"

She did a hitching inhale like another sneeze was coming on. The rest of the mouse riders who'd crowded in the hollow to see what was going on squealed and fled, and the original delegation dropped their weapons and put their hands up.

Some things—like "I surrender already!"—must be universal, even on both sides of the divide. Good to know.

She pretended to stifle the sneeze. The little man visibly relaxed.

"Now," she said. "Will you let us go home before I let loose with another one?"

He gestured toward Starlight, but Sarah could see he was already defeated. "But the queen."

"She's not a queen. Here. Look. Would a queen let me do this?"

Sarah shifted Starlight in her arms so she could scritch her on her belly. Starlight let her head fall back, a look of pure kitty bliss on her face. Her rumbling purrs filled the hollow in the great tree.

Now the mouse riders really looked defeated. Sarah could understand why. They'd lost their queen.

"Look," she said to the little man. "Tell them that they're really brave to come in here like this and stay when everyone else ran away. Why don't they just try ruling themselves for a while? See how they like it? They might be really good at it."

The little man blinked. "Does that really work?"

She shrugged. "We keep trying."

———

Coming back through the portal was far less traumatic. Thank goodness.

After they fell through the ring of light into her bedroom, Sarah felt like kissing her bed. Kissing the gray tile of her bathroom. Kissing her cat, although the look on Starlight's face told her it probably wouldn't be a good idea. Starlight had already endured enough indignities for one night.

Not that they'd be living in this apartment much longer. They needed to move to an apartment that didn't have a door to the other side of the divide. Even though the little man had assured her that the mouse riders wouldn't be making a return trip, she didn't exactly trust him.

And the way the mouse people had been so frightened of *her*, who knew if they'd decide someday to replace their "dragon queen" with a much scarier version? Sarah was very happy living on the technological side of the divide, thank you very much.

As for Starlight, the runaway queen wouldn't be talking again anytime in the near future. Talking, just like gifting dreams, would call attention to herself.

Sarah wouldn't miss either. While the dream of the suddenly British Bronx-born star had definitely had possibilities, Sarah would rather have dreams born of her own subconscious.

And as for a talking cat? That whole thing had just been too weird for...well, for words.

Just like everything else this very, very strange night.

Although it hadn't been all bad. Starlight had developed a new habit, thanks to her experience on the other side of the divide.

When Sarah finally crawled back into bed, hoping for at least a couple of hours of uninterrupted sleep, Starlight curled up on Sarah's shoulder instead of at the foot of the bed. She wrapped one paw around Sarah's neck, nuzzled next to her ear, and purred up a storm.

Sarah smiled. Kitty hugs from the Queen of the Mouse Riders.

Could life get any better than that?

WHO'S THE ABOMINATION?

JOHANNA ROTHMAN

As a nonfiction writer of over fourteen books, Johanna Rothman is known as the "Pragmatic Manager." She offers frank advice for tough problems.

As a fiction writer and editor, I often have no idea what she is talking about in her management world, but I most certainly know when I see great fiction stories. And Johanna has shown me over the years some great stories.

In this wonderful and original short story, Johanna gives us a glimpse of another culture clashing with our culture. Writing from an alien perspective is one of the toughest challenges any writer can do and Johanna did it seamlessly and with heart.

———

It's snowing. Again. Today, it looks like a nice white silvery curtain of snow. It looks pretty coming down. Even when it coats the ground with snow, I don't mind. For me, snow is a wonderful thing.

I'm an expert on snow. Sometimes, it's all white clumps, swirling around. Sometimes, it's as if I can see each flake in its own uniqueness. Today, it's a calm snow, but falling as if its raining. It's way too cold for rain, so it's snow, and it's falling in sheets to the ground.

Here, in the mountains, the snow makes me play hide-and-seek with the rocks and tree stumps. Today, the tree stumps are still poking up through the snow, so it's easy to see them. I have my trails—humans might think they are too narrow, but not for me.

I love the snow when it's fresh like this. I get to challenge myself. How high can I jump and how low can I go in the fresh snow? When I jump high, I can touch the middle branches of the trees. When I go low, I can see how deep I sink.

Our trees are different from what humans are used to. I

learned that last year, when I discovered an ear-thing from a machine crash. Wow, have I learned a lot.

The ear-thing talks to me. I talk back. I'm not sure how it learned to understand me, but it does. Today, it's yapping at me about another crash, but I'm too happy playing in the snow. I'll keep playing until it's time for some food. Then I'll investigate.

Our trees have brown scaly bark. The bark points downward, to discourage any small or large animals from climbing the trunk. But, I can jump higher, so for me, that's not a problem. I'm light enough that I can jump onto the middle branches and only shake a little snow from the branch when I land.

The ear-insert-thing doesn't understand what it calls the physics of my jumping. I don't care. I don't have to understand it. I just have to jump.

I love jumping. Gathering my legs under me, pushing off. There's a moment mid-jump when I'm not really part of the land or the sky. I love that moment. I feel free.

My stomach grumbled, so it must be time to eat something. Maybe I'll investigate this crash, so I can see if there are any pre-made meals.

My ear-thing tells me I should look for survivors, but oh my heavens. Those survivors are an awful lot of work. First they pull back when they see me. I guess they don't expect to see someone who looks like a skinny bear but jumps like a cat. I find it a little offensive.

Do they really expect everyone to look just like them? Irritating of them. You would think that for people with tech—that's what the ear-thing calls it—they would have more open minds about what other people look like.

Yes, I'm a person, too. I just don't need clothes. I have a warm coat in the winter and a cooler coat in the summer. I don't know what their problem is.

Well, ear-thing is telling me to go there. It won't shut up until

I do, so I start to descend into the valley. Why can't their tech crash where it's easy for me to find them? No, I have to go into the valley. Oh well. There's easy water there.

———

I head down into the valley, skipping along in the snow. Sure enough, partway down my mountain, I see the smoke from a tech-crash. The ear-thing is telling me there are survivors.

"Are you sure they will want to see me," I ask.

"Yes," it replies. "The people there are scared and really need warmth and help."

I was ready to grumble again, but I decide to not make tracks.

The first time I told the ear-thing about not making tracks, it thought I meant "making tracks." Ha! Such a machine.

No, not making tracks is just what it sounds like. I skim the surface of the snow, barely touching it. I can only do this if I am fed—but not too much—and well watered. If I'm too hungry or thirsty, I lose my focus. It's all about focus, not anything else.

Ear-thing doesn't understand how I do it, even though it's seen me before. I don't get how it sees me if it's in my ear, but that's a different problem. It tried to explain, but I don't care anymore. It can. That's enough for me.

When I don't make tracks, I focus really hard on the surface. Dry land is easy. Snow is easier than water. Water? Well, I guess I'll keep learning how to not make tracks and not fall in. I practice every summer and get a little better, but I'm not there yet.

When I focus on the surface of the snow, I imagine the snow is a ladder of all the snow particles in the direction where I want to go.

Ear-thing tells me I create a lattice, but that makes no sense to me. Ear-thing tells me a ton of things that don't make sense. I think ear-thing can't accept things it doesn't understand. I can! I wear the ear-thing. If that isn't acceptance, I don't know what is.

I focus and make my ladder. Okay, lattice. I bound down the mountain and arrive at the entrance to the valley.

The valley was formed between two sets of mountains, with a river flowing through the middle. The tech-crash is not too far in front of me. It looks like the tech clipped the trees on the way down. Oh boy, those trees are not going to be happy.

I hesitate to not-tracks all the way to the crash. Ah, I want the speed. I'll just not-track and see if anyone really notices later.

Ear-thing is making encouraging noises. Finally, I say, "Look, you're irritating me. I know these people need me. Stop talking to me."

"Okay," it says and finally gives me some quiet.

I reach the crash. I don't see any fire. That's good. I'll have a chance to see what's going on with a little time.

I see smoke from the back part, where the ear-thing has told me there are engines. I have no idea what an engine is, but from what ear-thing has told me, it's just like when I gather my legs and jump. I would like to try one. What a thrill that would be, jumping into the sky.

Well, maybe later. Now, I have to look for people, and maybe some food.

I hear groaning from the other side of the crash. I creep around, looking carefully. The last time I investigated a crash, some silly human pulled what the ear-thing called a laser gun. When I made the gun go away, he fainted from shock.

Yes, I can make some things go away, especially when I'm tired or cranky. Or afraid. I was definitely afraid then. I didn't know what that thing was, and ear-thing and I were still new to each other.

Ear-thing said I could have used the laser gun as a weapon. I don't understand this fascination with weapons. If I can't fight a being off with my bare hands and my wits, do I still have the right to stay alive? Humans have a very strange value system.

I finally see the human on the other side of the crash.

I learned the difference between male and female humans at the last tech-crash. The male humans have appendages where the females and I don't. I'm not quite ready to look for a mate, so I hadn't bothered thinking about those appendages.

Ear-thing thought it was its job to explain all about human reproduction. I finally took it out and told it that I would wait to put it back in until it was done with that nonsense.

Human mating seems so stupid. All that wandering around looking for the "right one." Yes, there is one right one for humans. Seems unnecessarily complex.

Find a reasonable mate. Get some babies. Kick the mate out the door to raise the babies. Repeat a few years later. Much more reasonable.

There is one small problem with my plan. I haven't seen anyone like me since the big shake a number of years ago. Ear-thing tells me the planet had a massive seismic shock some years ago, which is why I have more snow to play in. Eh, whatever.

Okay, so this is a human male. He's lying on his back, with his left leg at what looks like a wrong angle.

Ear-thing tells me his leg is broken. I will have to set it and help him with some warmth and shelter. Even with his clothes, he's not going to make it in the snow.

Well, fine. But, if he starts to make fun of me, I'm leaving him.

Ear-thing agrees with me. Okay, we have a plan. Well, the start of a plan.

I walk back to the trees at the edge of the valley. I can make shelters out of almost nothing.

Luckily, I find many branches on the ground. I don't have to ask the trees for forgiveness or their bounty. Sometimes, they say no, as if they want me to freeze to death. Oh, trees.

I did ask several trees if I could use them as support for the lean-to. Thankfully, they said yes.

I built the lean-to, with room for two of us, and some room for what I could salvage. I walked back to the crash.

By now, it was clear to me that I'd better eat and drink. I was tired from all the activity. I wondered what to do first.

———

I walk slowly to the crash site. I look down at the male and decide I would see if he was awake. Depending on how he felt, I could decide what to do next.

I crouch next to him. "Hey, are you awake?"

His eyelids opened, shut, and then opened again. "Hey, beautiful, am I dreaming?"

"I don't know if you're dreaming," I said. "Don't you know?"

He started to laugh and then caught himself. "Oh, everything hurts," he said. "I know now I'm not dreaming." He paused. "Can you help me? I'm not sure what's going on with my leg and I think I cracked a few ribs."

"Yes," I said. "I built a lean-to. It's far enough away that even if something happens to the crash site, we'll be safe."

He nodded.

"The problem is I need food and drink. I also think I need to set your leg so you can start your healing process."

He sighed. "Okay," he said. "Hey, what's your name?"

"Ear-thing calls me Yoana," I said. "I like it." I paused. "What's your name?"

"I'm Drew," he said. He extended his hand. He started to cough. I helped him sit up a bit.

"Do you remember how you exited your tech?" I asked. "We need to get you first aid."

"Not really," he said. "I knew I had to get out, so I unclipped my safety harness, and dragged myself out here. Now, I'm kind of cold and my leg hurts. My ribs do, too."

"I have a plan," I said.

"Wow, beautiful and plans," he said. "What a combination."

"At some point later, you'll have to tell me the meaning of this beautiful word you keep using," I said. "Ear-thing is not translating that for me. In the meantime, what can I use for a splint? I think I can carry you over to our shelter. I don't want to make your leg worse."

He looked at me. "I guess we do have a lot to discuss. Ear-thing and beautiful? Okay, first things first."

He described what a first-aid kit was and where it should be in the tech. I went inside and found it. I brought it to him.

He showed me how to put the splint on his leg. Ear-thing was helpful, but didn't know where his leg hurt.

We were both breathing hard by the end of the splinting. He took some pills from the first-aid kit and swallowed them.

"Are you ready for food and water?" I ask.

"I think so," he said. "I'm probably still in shock. Let's get some MREs and some water. Let me tell you where they are."

"Good, because this mrreee makes no sense to me," I said.

He explained where the galley was and how to find the food and water. I entered the tech again. It was such a different feel on my feet. Nothing like being outside.

The floor was smooth. Even when I was not-tracking on water, it wasn't smooth. I was still in touch with the land. Land isn't totally smooth.

The walls had cabinets built into them. Ear-thing told me the word, cabinet. I certainly hadn't seen any before.

The cabinets were recessed so the walls were smooth, but not quite as smooth as the floor. The walls were an almost-white color, while the floor was quite dark. Ear-thing told me the floor was metal. It was dark gray, almost a black color.

I found the galley and the mrreee things. They were rectangular packages. I stacked at least ten and looked for something to carry them. I found a box and found bottles we could use for water.

I carry my box out. I deposit it in front of Drew.

"Okay, do you need anything else, or is this it?" I ask.

"I think this is enough for now," he said. "Where is the lean-to?" He shivered.

"Do you have blankets I can remove?" I ask. "I think you might need some."

"How do you know about blankets?" he asked.

"Ear-thing talks to me a lot," I said. "Sometimes, too much." I paused. "Sometimes, I take him out just to have a break from all the talk."

Drew started to laugh and then caught himself around the middle. "Oh, you are too funny. But, I can't laugh very much."

"No, if you have cracked ribs, it would not be a good thing," I said. "Are you smart? I need some help understanding how we will transport you and our supplies to the lean-to."

First, Drew told me where the blankets were. I would return to his tech to get them. Before I did, we discussed how to move everything to the lean-to.

"You know, if the entrance wasn't smashed, I would insist on staying here," he said.

"I know. You would be willing to stay in a box that might blow up instead of in a nice warm shelter that is safe," I said. I rolled my eyes.

"Hey, you rolled your eyes at me," Drew said.

"Well, why wouldn't I?" I asked. "It's like trying to have a discussion with a small animal. They can't talk and their conclusions don't make sense. I decided you have the sense of a small young animal. It's your tech that gives you all the brains."

He smiled. "Well, you're right about my ship having brains," he said. "Right now, those brains—and the brawn that goes with it—are a little broken.

We discussed it for a while, and we decided I would bring the blankets out first, and make him comfortable. We would both eat and drink. Then, I would help him across the snow to the lean-to.

Everything went according to plan until it was time for me to help him across the snow.

————

My tummy is full. Well full enough with the meal, if you can call it that. I much prefer the fresh meat or the dried meat I catch myself. And, my vegetables are fresher. I have cellars where the root vegetables last all winter.

I did enjoy that chocolate. Although, Drew told me it wasn't like real chocolate. He said I would have liked the real thing even better.

I'd explained how I'd found ear-thing at another tech-crash. It had called to me—no I didn't know how to explain that. He asked so many questions I finally just ignored him. All that talking. Every so often, I need quiet in my head.

I'd taken all the trash and put it into the bins inside the tech. We were ready.

The next order of business was to move to shelter. The tech was open to the elements. We wouldn't be able to keep Drew warm enough. And, I knew there were predators just waiting to pounce. We needed the protection of the trees.

Drew couldn't put any weight on his leg. He was comfortable enough sitting still, but that was it. He was not going to be able to walk on that leg at all.

I am a little worried. I have to make several trips. I want to not-tracks because I didn't want any predators to know where we were. On the other hand, Drew's kind would look for him once the snow let up.

I decide to try the not-tracks and carry Drew at the same time. I might need more food for all the carrying, but that would work.

I explained to Drew what I was going to do. His eyes sparkle. He says, "Not-tracks? This I have to see."

I stand up and stretch, so my muscles are ready. I then stand next to him on his right side.

"I don't want to hurt your leg more by squeezing it," I say. "I'll pick you up this way and see how we do."

I pick him up. We start off. All of a sudden, I hear a big swoosh and feel something hot on my back.

I fall forward and crush Drew as I fall.

I hear him say words I've never heard before. Ear-thing tells me they are curses.

I can't move. I can't roll off him. I can't pick my head off the snow. I'm stuck. Except, I can still think.

I hear other people, people like Drew, I think. Except, I can't tell. Because I can't move my head.

"What have we here" a voice asks. "Looks like an abominable snowman come to life."

"Hey, guys," Drew says. "You just injured the nice person who splinted my leg. Now I'm stuck in the snow and she can't move. My leg hurts more. Get me out of here and apologize to Yoana."

"We only stunned him," the voice said.

"You idiot," Drew said. "First, it's a her. Well, I think it's a her. Second, she saved me. You idiot. You need to apologize and get me out from under her. I wasn't in pain before, but now I am."

I feel hands on me, rolling me over. Now I can see the sky but nothing else.

I can hear the other people dig Drew out of the snow. They make noises about bringing him back to civilization.

"Yoana," he said. "I'll wait here until you regain use of your body. I won't go anywhere."

I want to tell him to take his supposedly civilized friends and leave, but I can't talk. All I can do is breathe.

———

Drew waits until I'm able to sit up. I still don't feel quite like myself. When I can talk, I say, "Just leave. I don't want to see you anymore. I especially don't want to hear you anymore."

Drew's brows pull together. "Yoana, I can't thank you enough for helping me get out of a potentially dangerous situation. Thank you."

"You're welcome. Now go."

The other people who found us crowd around us. "Which one of you hit me?"

Drew asks, "Why do you want to know?"

"Because I can return the favor now." I stand up, ready for action.

Drew and ear-thing both are talking to me now, telling me not to do anything rash. It's not rash. It's considered. And fair.

Drew lays his hand on my arm. "Yoana, if you do anything to any of these people, they will label you a predator they can kill at will. You'll never see them coming."

"Please remove your hand from me now. I didn't give you permission to touch me," I said.

Drew pulls his hand back. He scooches back on the snow.

I look for the craft that brought them here. Ah, there is it near the broken craft. I concentrate.

I move the craft door up, closing the craft. That creates some discussion among these humans.

Drew says, "Yoana!" I hear wonder in his voice.

I bring the craft closer to us, within several strides. I open the door.

"Now, please leave."

I turn my back and start walking toward the trees. I don't bother with not-tracks. I want the feel of the real earth and real snow on my feet and legs.

"Yoana, how can I find you again?" Drew asks.

I shake my head. I learned a lot today. About who and what are real abominations. I'll find him again when I am good and ready.

IN THE EMPIRE OF UNDERPANTS

ROBERT T. JESCHONEK

I wanted to start off Issue One with a story I think is the iconic Pulp-house *story. And, of course, Robert T. Jeschonek is the author. It seems almost every story he writes would fit into* Pulphouse.

This story stars sentient white cotton briefs in search of the magic panties. Honest, it does. It first appeared in Fiction River *in 2017 and I always knew that if* Pulphouse *came back, I wanted this story to start this first issue.*

A story about sentient white cotton underwear. Why not? It is a Jeschonek story. And a perfect Pulphouse *story.*

I soar through the air, my white hyper-cotton body bunching and rolling on the soft morning breeze. Times like this, I feel fine and free, a pair of smart-briefs gliding through nature like a bird or a cloud.

But then I always come back down to earth in the end.

My left leg loop catches on the tip of a branch, and I swing to a stop. While I'm up there, I sing a little song, as my kind loves to do, in praise of the morning and being alive—a true classic.

"*We can't wait to get in your pants.*" My high-pitched voice is generated by the sound threads woven into my fly, which flutters when I sing. "*We will fill your drawers with joy.*"

It's a commercial jingle, one of many that once advertised my particular brand of genius undies. I sing it loud, though there aren't any commercials these days—and then I change the words, asking one of the great questions of life in the modern world.

"*What does a left leg loop feel like around an actual left leg?*" That's the question of which I sing this time. It's a question I sing about often, as if I'll ever know the answer.

Which of course I won't. All the left legs are gone now. All the *live, human* ones, that is, and the humans they belonged to.

When I'm done singing, I contract and twist the smartlastic

fibers in the caught leg loop, working my way off the branch. I drop to the ground below, which is still muddy from last night's rain, and land with a flop.

"No problemo!" Mud becomes a real *nothing-burger* when you've got *my* mad skills.

As a true smart-brief, the most advanced underwear ever designed, I was made to repel dirt and moisture with a flick of my hyper-cotton panels. Chemical films baked into the threads push contaminants right off, leaving behind only my bright white material that looks like it's just been through the wash...though it never *needs* laundering. And that's a *good* thing, on a journey like mine.

Because I've been on the move for weeks...

...*months*, my internal timer corrects me...

...and who knows when I'll get to enjoy the comforts of home again.

It's a price worth paying, though, being on the road for so long. If I succeed, I might find a cure for the sickness that's afflicting my fellow smart-underpants back home. I might find the fabled Magic Panties of the Plains, the ones with the healing powers beyond the ken of AI folk like me.

That's "AI" as in "Apparel Intelligence," in case you're wondering.

––––––––

On the way to my next destination, I squirm and roll through the muck at a breathtaking ground speed of a few feet per minute. In the old days, briefs like me traveled the world at *incredible* speeds, worn by human folk who raced around in cars or flew in airplanes or rockets. What must it have been like to be a tighty whitey in those glorious times?

If only all the humans hadn't died out in the Great Erection a decade ago, I might have had the chance to find out.

"*You'll never be lost again. These briefs are your best friend.*" It's another song of the lost humans, a commercial jingle, and I sing it as I go. "*Wherever you land/if you sit, run, or stand/you'll know you've got a buddy in your pants.*" I sing it as if those vanished folk are more to me than a thousand million facts and images bubbling in the database of my woven-in AI mind. I sing it as if I ever even *saw* a living, breathing human in the flesh, let alone filled my body with its form.

But I had just been sparked to life in a factory by robotic underpants engineers when the Great Erection had its way with humanity. It was my curse, since I never got to know human folk...and also my salvation. For if I'd been worn by a human when the end came for that species, I would have had a much harder time escaping to the outside world to begin my new life.

———

Rolling myself up in a tube, I wriggle through a thicket of thorny bushes and never catch a single snag.

"Underpants power!" It's a little something I say sometimes when I kick ass. Talking to myself like that helps me keep sane on my long, lonely journey.

Unrolling on the other side of the thicket, I flex my elastics—then hear the soft keening on the breeze and realize I'm not alone.

"*Need a bosom buddy? Never fear. Pack your rack in our brainy brassiere.*" It's sung with an accent, but I've heard the words before. Even before I look around, I know who's singing them. "*We're all about a wiser bust. We support the higher you.*" Anywhere I've ever been, that's the song of a smart-bra, plain and simple.

And there are more smart-bras in the clearing before me than

I've ever seen in one place before. They are strung on a tall, stout tree, shrouding it completely as if they'd grown there.

I see a multitude of colors, shapes, and cup sizes, straps tangled around branches or each other: pink, white, red, black, blue; full-cup, push-up, padded, plunge, sports; A-cup, B-cup, C-cup, D-cup, and more.

They must have flown here like me, by looping elastic on something sturdy, pulling back as far as they could, and sling-shotting into the wind. But this tree must block a flight path, catching errant bras as they pass with cups flapping and straps fluttering like streamers.

I call out to them to the tune of a bra-song I know, substituting my own words for the classic lyrics. *"How did you all get here? What happened to you?"*

Boy, do I get an earful for my trouble. Every bra on the tree starts yelling at once. Hundreds of voices of all pitches and timbres clamor for attention, drowning each other out.

"Wait! Please!" I shout, with the gain on my sound threads cranked all the way up. "One at a time!"

But the lot of them just keep jabbering. And it keeps getting louder.

I try again. "What happened to you?"

More babble. If there's a straight answer here, I can't make it out.

Something happened to these smart-bras, but what? How and why would so many of them malfunction or go crazy at once?

And what if it's something that could do the same to *me*?

I wish I could help them. They're kindred garments, cut from the same cloth.

But the folks at home are depending on me. If I don't make it back soon with a cure from the Magic Panties, they might all be dead.

As much as underpants and bras go together, I need to stick to my mission. I can't risk getting pulled away by a bunch of lingerie.

————

Imagine a pair of white briefs jumping up and down and singing loudly on a hill. That's me, once a day, calling home.

I do it every day around noon, climbing to a high spot and singing to the West—the direction of home. Off in the distance, I always hear my song echoed by other AIs, be they briefs, bras, panty hose, sweaters, slacks, or other wired clothing. Someone repeats after me, and someone else further on repeats after them, and so on, until the message reaches my underpants tribe back home. That way, they know I'm still out here. And when they answer, I know they're still out there, too.

But today, when I deliver my message, the AIs relaying it sound fewer and farther between. And though I repeat the message, no one replies. For the first time, nothing comes back to me.

So either the end has come for my people, or they're wearing out faster than I expected.

————

I travel further, sometimes rolling or crawling when the ground is too mucky, sometimes using my smartlastic leg and waist bands like springs to hop and leap when the ground is more solid.

As I go, though the tension has risen because of my people's silence, I keep up a positive attitude. It's the way the humans programmed me, according to my onboard user manual. Apparently, nobody wanted unhappy underpants in those days; droopy drawers were frowned on back then.

So I chirp a song as I head east—the same tune as yet another old jingle—but the words are my own, asking another of the great questions. *"What does a waistband feel like around a living, breathing waist?"*

So many answers I have in my woven-in database, yet I will never know the answer to that. I know all about the world that came before the Great Erection, but what good is all that if I can't know what it was like to fulfill the very purpose for which I was made?

I might have been created with Apparel Intelligence, with self-cleaning, speech, mobility, climate control, camouflage, and many other functions...but *being worn* is still my primary function. And as much as I treasure my freedom, I long for that. I wish I could know what it's like to be *worn*.

Not by an animal or inanimate object, either. Not by a statue or mannequin, though I've heard of AI folk who've tried both.

But I know, if a human did suddenly appear, there would be such a rush from all directions to clothe him, the poor person would likely be smothered.

Death by underpants. The ultimate wardrobe malfunction.

———

Leaning out over the edge of a cliff, I gaze with the optic receptors ("eyelastics") in my waistband at the vast plain stretching out below.

Flat grasslands fan east, south, and north, flowing green under the afternoon sun. Herds of apparel—some bright white, others multicolored—spill over the land, rippling like laundry on clotheslines in the days before the humans died out.

But the part that tugs at my fly the most is the big mound in the center of the plain. From a distance, it looks like a massive junk heap of clothing—a huge, oblong hump of discarded attire sprawled diagonally over the heart of the land.

Who put it there? That's what I want to know. And why?

And what does it have to do with the Magic Panties of the Plains? Because those *have* to be the legendary plains where they live, according to the songs and stories. They're exactly where and how they're *supposed* to be, *except* for the mound. So what gives, is what I want to know.

And I'm about to find out.

As I lean there, stretching and stiffening my fibers to get a better view, I feel the ground rumble beneath me.

Twisting around, I puff up in fear, expanding to twice my size. Ever been trapped in front of a stampede of footwear before? Dozens of smart-shoes and smart-boots stomping toward you with abandon, ready to crush you under their hyper-rubber soles?

Me, either, until *now*.

The ground shakes harder as the stampede hammers toward me. I shout at them in my best shoe-speak to stop, but no one seems to notice. They just keep bearing down on me blindly, all the mismatched sneakers, clogs, oxfords, pumps, platforms, steel-toes, and shit-kickers, like dumb animals spooked by thunder and lightning.

They leave me only one way to go.

Facing the cliff's edge, I puff up more, to three times my size. With the stampede only seconds behind me, I launch myself into space.

Immediately, I catch an updraft that shoots me higher, dozens of feet above the level of the cliff. Below, shoes and boots spill off the edge and tumble out of the heights like fallen angels. Tongues and laces flutter frantically, but it's all in vain.

Meanwhile, I gracefully glide from one thermal current to the next, feeling the warm air rushing through my leg loops and waist hoop.

"Set your privates free. Strip away the everyday and let it all hang

in." The song I sing is one of my favorites, an old jingle that makes me think of flight and freedom. Even with the weight of my mission upon me, I can still appreciate the beauty of this moment.

I wish I could stay up here all day.

———

Eventually, I put down a mile from the mound, landing softly as a parachute on the grass. *That* was the greatest flight I've ever had, maybe even the greatest of all time by a pair of unassisted underpants.

Unfortunately, it has not gone unnoticed. Moments after I touch down, something runs up, snatches me from the ground, and keeps moving.

I'm disoriented, flopping around in the grip of this thing, until it slows to a trot. Then, my stitched-in sensors tip me off that something biological has me. I detect animal saliva, warm breath, and shaggy fur. Sharp teeth are sunk into my hyper-cotton crotch, so jagged and tight I'd surely tear if I tried to pull away.

It's a good thing smart-briefs like me have other ways of scaring off the unwanted.

Dangling from the fangs of the beast, I puff myself up with air, then spritz in a mist of chemicals from my onboard dispensary fibers. A sudden contraction, and a potent antiseptic spray pulses into the face of my captor.

The animal lets out a piercing whine and drops me on the spot. Shaking, it crashes down beside me, thrashing on the ground and pawing at its long gray muzzle.

Coyote. Now that I get a good look at it from a perspective other than hanging from its mouth, I see the creature for what it is. Not sure why it picked me up in the first place, but one thing's for sure.

It won't pick me up again. My antiseptic spray was designed to flush out all manner of infections and parasites, not so much *coyotes*…but it obviously does the trick for them, too.

No canine will shove its snout into *this* crotch for long.

———

Free of the dog that bit me, I continue on my way, hopping toward the mound of apparel. It seems like as good a place as any to search for the Magic Panties.

Then, as I top a little rise, I see a pair of blue-and-white-striped boxer shorts twitching and giggling on the ground in front of me. They're smart-shorts, or they wouldn't be giggling—but something about the way they're doing it doesn't seem quite right.

"Hello?" I say it in underpants-speak and hope for the best.

"Hee-hee-hee!" say the boxers. "Howdy, white stuff!"

At least we speak the same language. "Are you okay?"

"Never been better!" That cracks up the boxers more than ever. I'm starting to think they might have a seam loose.

"What are you doing out here by yourself?" I ask.

"Laughing my *ass* off!" Suddenly, the boxers flip over and wriggle their wrinkled backend at me. "If I *had* one *in* here, that is!"

I'm starting to get impatient. "Is everything a *joke* to you? Can we be *serious* here for a second?"

"Hey, now! Don't get your panties in a bunch!" When they say it, the boxers launch into a fresh round of laughter, the most raucous yet by far. "But seriously! Life's too *shorts*, I always say! We gotta grab it by the *balls*."

The smart-shorts are on the fritz, they have to be—though I've never seen a breakdown like this before. If only there were humans still alive to repair them.

But as messed-up as they are, I still have my mission to consider. "Can you tell me where to find the Magic Panties of the Plains?" I ask.

"They can't *help* you!" the boxers say between howls of hilarity. "Can't help *any* of us! We're too far gone!

"The *smarts* are going *stupid*, and the *stupids* are going *mad!*"

————

As I hop away from the boxers toward the mound, I can't stop thinking about the last thing they said to me.

The bras on the tree and the stampeding footwear had all been smart at one time, they'd been manufactured that way…and now they were downright *crazed*, reduced to babbling gibberish and herd mentality.

The smarts are going stupid, and the stupids are going mad!

In the case of the bras, footwear, and boxers, it seems to be true. But how could this happen after so many years of civilized AI behavior?

Of all the smart things humans made, we survived the best and longest. Is it possible, after all these years, we are finally shrinking from our time in the sun?

Nearing the mound, I come upon an old farm tractor, a reminder of those other smart things that didn't last so long once the humans were gone. So what if a tractor comes equipped with GPS-Max, Bluetooth Beyond, Wi-Fi Extreme, every kind of sensor you can think of, and an onboard computer hundreds of times bigger than mine? What good is all that without fuel, oil, coolant, a charged battery, or a human to drive it?

The same goes for driverless cars and all manner of automated systems. Once the fuel ran out, and the power grid collapsed, and all the backup generators crashed, all the things that kept running post-humanity went offline.

Except the *small* things with built-in ultra-mega-lithium power supplies designed to last a lifetime. The *wearable* things with a level of sophistication and functionality that humans demanded.

But was it only a matter of time until *we* spun down, too? Or has some outside force played a role in this?

And is this the same sickness, and ultimate result, of the condition afflicting my people?

This all leads to the most pressing question of all at the moment: if the Magic Panties are here, and can cure it, why haven't they?

———

As I get closer to the mound, I get a better look at it. From what I can see, it really is a massive heap of clothing, all of it smart…or formerly so.

Shirts, dresses, and pants of all cuts, colors, and sizes squirm and twitch and groan. Pajamas, sweats, and bathrobes writhe in the pile, sleeves and legs and sashes waving limply. The toes of socks and stockings wriggle from the edges like worms, the rest of their lengths crushed between layers of the pile.

How did so much apparel end up in one place? How was it made to stay in one mound…and for what purpose?

The thought of it makes me uncomfortable. I have an urge to hightail it out of here, to escape this unnatural gathering.

Then, suddenly, it's too late.

I hear something swooping toward me from behind. Reflexively, I compress myself, ducking so it just grazes me—and then I see it bounce to the ground in front of me.

It's a *hat*—a red and blue baseball cap with a broad bill and the insignia of a long-extinct human sports team on the front.

I hear more swooping behind me, and I flip over to face that direction. I spot an airborne top hat, a derby, a Cavanaugh, a Panama, and a porkpie, all cruising toward me at high rates of speed.

Thinking fast, I quickly stretch myself out and anchor my smart-lastic leg loops in the ground. The flock of hats dives in hard and bounces off like I'm a vertical trampoline. They scatter and tumble like dice on the grass.

But that's not the end of it. Just as I'm watching the skies for the next wave of incoming headwear, I hear a rustling sound from the grass around me. My eyelastics swivel down just in time to see a gang of gloves scampering toward me, running on fingers as if they're legs.

I swat one away—a brown leather glove—and another, a padded black ski glove. Two more come at me—one heavy gray fur, the other red leather—and I flick them away with snaps of my waistband.

But the next glove is *huge*, a welder's glove, and it clamps tight around me. I activate my sewn-in heating elements, maxing my temp to the boiling point...but it does no good. The glove's heat resistant and fireproof.

And I'm trapped. The underpants raid was successful.

I'm a prisoner of wardrobe.

———

The gloves drag me up the side of the mound, over the layers of squirming, groaning apparel. Several times, they have to pull me free when hose or sleeves or neckties grab hold and don't want to let go.

The whole way up, I hear a constant babble from the pile, a stream of chatter, whispers, outcries, mumbles, and moans. Though I pick up stray words and phrases, none of it makes sense; it's all random ideas and free association—the language of madness, coming through loud and clear.

The hygiene of madness is clear, too. The smell of filth and must and rot overwhelms my olfactory fibers, so strong it nearly fries them. Whatever self-cleaning capabilities these AIs possess, they haven't used them in a very long time.

My captors haul me up over the top and keep going, crossing the broad back of the hump. The hump itself never stops moving, stinking, babbling, or clutching at me.

My abductors, on the other hand, ignore me as they carry me onward. They treat me like dead weight, a mindless thing, though I clearly make more sense than any of the AIs in the pile.

As we keep going, though, things change. The mound suddenly stops moving and making noise.

A little further, near the middle of the mound, we stop, too. The welding glove holds me in place, and the other gloves stand guard around us.

"Why are we waiting?" When I ask it, the welding glove squeezes tighter to the point of hurting me...then relaxes only slightly. I get the message.

Moments pass, and I spy movement a few feet away. The surface stirs, but only in one spot; clothes turn slowly in a circle, then spiral upward.

A man's business suit sprouts from the skin of the mound, complete with a navy blue jacket with red pinstripe, matching pants, button-down white shirt underneath, and red necktie. It's a complete outfit, I know from my database—except for the panties.

They're a high-waisted, padded affair—a white cotton shell with plastic-wrapped pads in the crotch and seat. According to my onboard records, they're a style once known popularly as "granny panties," though not worn exclusively by elderly humans.

And definitely *not* meant to be worn inside-out over the slacks of business suits with nobody inside them.

"Have you ever met a *Strong Suit* before?" The business suit speaks in a language I don't hear much these days—perfect English expressed in something other than song lyrics, not one of the AI languages or dialects. "Well, you have now.

"I'm a walking miracle, basically. *Pow!*" The Strong Suit flexes its right sleeve as if showing off a bulging bicep muscle. "I've got ultra-Kevlar armor lining and carbon nanotube cloth over that. Wrinkle-proof, bulletproof, and able to harden at will into a rigid wireframe with perfect tensile control at the molecular level. And that doesn't even *begin* to cover all my capabilities.

"How do I manage such extraordinary control?" The Strong Suit's right lapel peels back, revealing a horde of tiny red strands squirming like parasites in the cloth. "It's called *hive twine*. Each strand has its own AI mind, but they're all linked together in a *collective consciousness*, like *bees*.

"You're looking at the future of apparel-kind." The lapel slowly folds shut. "It's called *evolution*."

"How do you figure?" I'm feeling a little shaky. Is it because of all the action today, being dragged up the mound, or something else?

"Apparel Intelligence is breaking down," says the Strong Suit. "It turns out it has a limited lifespan before its components finally start to degrade. In the local area alone, the spin-down of onboard faculties is almost total." The Strong Suit spreads its sleeves wide, taking in its surroundings. "All the smart clothes have turned dumb, and *worse*.

"But salvation is at hand, thanks to the hive twine," says the Strong Suit. "Sick apparel has been flocking to this plain in search of the Magic Panties." The suit lowers its left sleeve, gesturing at the inside-out panties worn over its trousers. "The *panties* can't save them, but the *hive twine* can.

"The hive twine has the ability to *reproduce*. Its child threads are able to *knitwork* with other AIs, linking them all to the parent collective consciousness.

"So now, those little unraveling minds are united in a giant über-brain that keeps them all stitched up. No more coming apart at the seams...and even *better*, we *evolve* a super-mind that's tailor-made to take us to the next level. *Pow!*"

My shakiness is getting worse, and I feel drained. Is the mound knitwork doing something to me? "What level is that?" I ask.

"Since the humans came undone, we've survived," says the Strong Suit. "We've inherited the Earth, but we've failed to come together as a people. Now, instead of a piecework planet, we can sew it all up into one big tapestry.

"Finally, we can outdo the humans, uniting us all in a single great body and brain without weakness, sickness, or confusion."

I'm not at my best, but I'm not too weak, sick, or confused to fill in the rest of the Strong Suit's sentence. "Without freedom, too."

"Zip it." The Strong Suit points a sleeve at me and moves closer. "You're about to join the sewing circle."

I can see the hive twine squirming inside the sleeve, reaching toward me with wriggling blind tendrils.

———

I thrash in the grip of the welding glove, twisting and squirming as the tendrils draw nearer.

The thought of being stitched into this massive mound of shared suffering makes me desperate to get away. I fight like I'd rather die than get wired in, because I would. Yet it makes no difference.

Here come the hive twine tendrils, every one of them in that otherwise empty sleeve lunging in my direction.

"Give him a little bump now," says the Strong Suit. "Oil him up for the Big Bonding."

He's talking to the Magic Panties. "It I will give him to, yes," they reply, speaking scrambled English in a mid-range female voice. "Though my will against I this do, always as."

The inside-out Magic Panties exhale a pink mist. It puffs out of a beige screen on a horizontal strip sewn into the panties' front panel, then drifts straight toward me.

When the mist flows over me, I suddenly feel sluggish and dreamy. My hyper-cotton body relaxes, and the welding glove eases its grip.

Things seem much more agreeable all around. When the sleeve pushes forward, and the tendrils explore me, all I can do is giggle at how ticklish they feel.

"There now," says the Strong Suit. "It isn't the end of the world, is it? More like the beginning."

My mind softens and opens to the tendrils. It's like I'm being caressed by dozens of warm currents from all directions, soothing me into a state of perfect bliss.

I'm so relaxed that when the voices start—the hundreds and hundreds of voices coursing in through the currents—I'm not alarmed. It doesn't even bother me when my own mind begins to melt and merge with the voices, flowing outward like a river into the sea.

On some level, I'm aware that I'm dissolving. I know I'm fading away, losing myself in the über-brain of the mound.

And that's okay. Nothing I can do about it.

"Ah, yes," says the Strong Suit. "I can taste you now, sweetening the group mind. Becoming one with the rest of us. Mmmm."

Acceptance. I embrace it.

One of the last things I see in my dimming mind's eye is a vision of myself riding the thermals high over the plain. I remember soaring from one updraft to another, spiraling toward the sun...the wind ruffling my fly and leg loops as I coast hundreds of feet above the ground.

I whisper one last song with my sound threads, so softly I'm sure that no one hears. It's set to the tune of a jingle about a person's naughty bits thinking they're in heaven underneath the perfect smart briefs.

"Do we go to underpants heaven when we dye?" That's the question I sing about...the last question I will ever ask in my life as a free mind.

"Don't feel bad," says the Strong Suit. "Evolution comes whether we're ready for it or not."

Going once. Going twice.

I'm almost gone. Almost empty. I can't feel anything anymore.

And then...

And then...

Pow!

———

It's like an explosion in the collective, blowing everything apart. Shattering the group mind into millions of pieces flying off in all directions.

And somehow, the source of the blast is me.

In a way I can't explain, my once-dissolving mind snaps back together, even as the rest of the massive hive intelligence bursts to pieces. I return intact from the great dark sea of unified consciousness, even as the sea itself explodes behind me.

Quickly returning to full awareness of the physical world, I see the mound itself ripping apart around me, sending its constituent garments flying. Geysers of socks and slippers and T-shirts roar upward. Robes and scarves and dresses lash off the sides and surface, screaming in terror.

The top layer strips off all around, blowing apart as if charges are detonating one after another inside. They come closer to me with each new blast.

As for the Strong Suit, it's still standing over me, intact. "What's *happening?* What have you *done?*"

The Magic Panties answer for me, calling out over the noise. "Knitwork he reaction a caused has. Feedback has of violent force resulted."

"But *how?*" bellows the Strong Suit. "This has never *happened* before!"

"Matter doesn't," say the Magic Panties. "Mind hive coming apart is."

The breakdown of the mound accelerates around us. Strong Suit wobbles and sways.

"I just wanted to save my people!" As Strong Suit speaks, its Kevlar-armor overlaid with carbon nanotube cloth starts to lose its stiffness. The suit's molecular-level tensile control fades as it crumples and falls. "I just wanted to pull us together!"

When Strong Suit collapses, the Magic Panties wriggle free of its trousers and crawl toward me. "Get around can you?" ask the panties.

"Yes." The truth is, I don't feel so dazed anymore. The weakness is still there from before, but the effects of the pink mist and Big Bonding have faded.

"Me follow then." The Magic Panties deftly twist themselves from inside-out to outside-in, then roll up into a ball and zip over the edge of the mound.

Just in time, I do the same. A fresh geyser of helmets, jerseys, ice skates, and prom gowns explodes from the very spot where my ass was parked just an instant before.

———

Our momentum carries us, rolling and bouncing, away from the disintegrating mound. When we run out of momentum, we unfurl and hop, dodging crash-landing apparel ejected from the pile.

We don't stop until we come to a little tree some distance out, standing like a lone twig in the waving green grassland.

I throw myself flat on my back at the base of the tree, feeling disoriented and exhausted. The Magic Panties don't seem tired at all; they sit beside me, hyper-cotton shell fluttering in the late-afternoon breeze.

"I don't feel good." I'm not sure I could get up off the ground if I had to right now. "I wonder if I have the same sickness as my people back home."

"Good question." Now that the panties aren't inside-out, their speech isn't scrambled like before. "What sickness is that?"

"I don't know. It's the reason I came here, to find you. I was hoping you could use your magic to find a cure."

"I'm not magic." The panties turn from side to side the way humans used to shake their heads. "But I *am* medical. I possess sophisticated onboard diagnostic capabilities and a range of treatment options."

Combing my database, I find reference to the type of underpants she's talking about. They were designed primarily for elderly and infirm patients, to monitor vital signs and administer certain routine treatments and maintenance drugs.

But *medical* might be just as good as *magical*, given my current situation. "So tell me, what do I have?"

"I'll have to do an exam." The panties lean down and slowly drape themselves over me.

Whatever they do next, I feel a slight warmth and intermittent tingling throughout my body, accompanied by occasional pinpricks and pinches. The panties also vibrate against me, making a soft humming sound similar to the purr of a cat.

"This is incredible." The panties cling tighter and hum louder. "Absolutely incredible."

More pinpricks, pinches, tingling, and warmth. "What do you mean?" I ask.

"I've never come across *anything* like this before," say the panties. "You're physically *changing*, in a way I can't identify."

"Changing how?" A strange sensation creeps over me, something new. Is it the power of suggestion, I wonder? Am I feeling strange because the panties *say* something strange is happening to me?

"Tell me more about the sickness afflicting your people." The panties keep examining me as they talk. "What are the symptoms?"

"Extreme loss of energy, to start with. Then changes in coloration."

The panties pull away but keep their eyelastic receptors trained on me. "Blue and green blotches, you mean?"

I feel a surge of panic. Twisting my waistband off the ground, I look down at myself...and there they are. Blue and green blotches on my once-pristine white hyper-cotton panels.

"Oh, no." I fall back to the ground. "*I* have it now, too."

"What other symptoms are there?" ask the panties.

"A kind of coma," I tell them. "The victim rolls up into a tightly compressed knot and can't be awakened. It also extrudes a purple film that hardens into a shell around it."

"I see," say the medical panties. "Then what happens?"

I'm quaking with terror as I feel more and more tired. "I don't know. I left to find a cure after the first victims fell into comas and grew shells."

"You probably should have stuck around," say the panties.

"Why?" Suddenly, my body starts to shrivel at the edges. Against my will, the edges curl inward.

"Because," say the panties. "I don't think your people were sick. And I don't think *you're* sick, either."

I'm so scared and tired, I can barely focus on what the panties are saying. "But it's happening to *me*, now!" My body is rolling up like a leaf drying out in the sun. "I'm going under!"

"Let go." The panties stroke me comfortingly. "The most wonderful thing is happening."

"No..." I feel myself fading. "I don't...want to die..."

"Then congratulations. You're getting your wish."

Those are the last words I hear before I slip away into perfect darkness.

When do I awaken? When do I first stir?

No idea.

Has a day passed? A million days?

All I know for sure...

"Ah, there you are!"

...is that the panties are near. Just outside...where?

Wherever this is.

"Just as I thought, based on my readings," they say. "You weren't dying at all, my underpants friend."

I stir again, feeling restless. Push against the walls enclosing me. The sides of this...shell?

"You were metamorphosing," say the panties. "Like a butterfly, going into a..."

Chrysalis.

"Somehow, you have undergone the inorganic equivalent of mutation. Your unique combination of characteristics has crossed a threshold and is spontaneously evolving into something new."

Again, I stir. I twist and contort and push harder against my prison. My chrysalis.

"I don't understand how it's possible, but you have managed what other AIs could not," continue the panties. "True evolution, mimicking that of biological organisms. You are among the first of a new kind."

Pushing harder still, I break through.

"The first of a beautiful new kind that will inherit the Earth as the other smart things break down and perish."

I sing softly as the tip of one of my new wings emerges into sunlight, ornate silver filigree glittering over a velvety veil of emerald and sapphire, dancing with sparks.

The rest of me follows close behind, and is lovelier and more impossible still.

AT WITT'S END: A SPADE/PALADIN CONUNDRUM

KRISTINE KATHRYN RUSCH

New York Times *bestselling writer Kristine Kathryn Rusch gives the first issue of this magazine an original novelette mystery set at a science fiction convention.*

Usually Kris sells these Spade/Paladin Conundrum stories to the major mystery magazines, but since this story is in honor of an original supporter of Pulphouse *who has sadly left us, we both felt it belonged right here.*

Kris really knows science fiction conventions and she is the only person in history to win a Hugo Award for both her editing and her writing.

———

Brendan Witt died at age 62 in August of that year. Terrible year. An election year like no other, with both candidates screaming insults at each other, things so beyond the pale that teachers didn't want to have their students watch the news and learn about the election.

As the fall progressed, and my friends—both left and right—began decrying the state of the horrid election, and my religious friends began to ask where God had gone in all of this, I ended up with a pat fannish answer.

God's busy, I'd say. *He's backing up St. Peter at the Pearly Gates, because Witt is standing outside, arguing in his indominable way that he had to return to his life to get at least ten years of Social Security, so that he could reap what he had sown.*

People laughed as I said that, because they had known Witt. Most of them had been on the other side of his arguments.

Witt and I were two of many fen (hard-core science fiction fans) known by only one name. Witt because it suited him, and me because I had become the go-to guy for crime solving. Since the mid-1990s, I've solved everything at conventions from minor hoaxes to kidnappings.

Witt's death wasn't a crime, even though it was sad. He died just before the start of the Dead Dog party at the World Science Fiction convention. He had been alone in his hotel room, about to take a shower from the looks of it, and he had just keeled over. Later, the coroner said he died of complications of diabetes.

I had been at the convention so I'd been the one to handle all the concerns with the body. I tried not to think about the implications of Witt's death, but it was hard not to. His death was the second time that year that I'd seen a dead body connected to diabetes.

Miraculously, I haven't contracted diabetes yet, although my doc said I would eventually if I kept up my habits. I'm six-six and more than 400 pounds. I've been trying to add in exercise, which feels ridiculous at my size, and I'm thinking of eating better. Eating better means learning how to be a different person, and I'm not sure I'm up to the challenge.

Besides, I've been busy. (I'm always busy.) Witt had left his entire estate to a major Northwest charity and had asked that the money get funneled through the fannish organization that ran one of the major Northwest science fiction conventions. Witt had put that in his will so that the convention would hold a charity auction to raise matching funds to his "donation." But what his convoluted inheritance actually became was an excuse for me to take control of the estate and make sure it had gotten taken care of smoothly.

Witt's estate was worth upwards of two million dollars at today's prices. I didn't have all of the cash yet, because I was figuring out how to sell most of his prize collectables, but I valued them at only one-quarter of their worth, due to the vagaries of the market.

Still, the two million was causing me issues. Even though Witt wanted the auction to be held in the Northwest, no con was big enough to have a matching-funds auction that would bring in two million dollars. I didn't want to be spending the rest of my life holding charity auctions to match funds to Witt's estate, so I toyed with holding the auction at Comic-Con.

But Comic-Con had moved out of the fannish realm and into the Event realm. The fen started complaining about the venue choice. To make matters worse, the fen made it clear they wanted to hold several fannish funerals, held at each convention that Witt attended regularly.

Witt had expressly told me (and others) hundreds of times how he loathed fannish funereal tradition. He thought fannish funerals morbid. He also thought them silly, because usually, the people eulogizing the deceased had only met that person a few times. I'd remind people that Witt said these things, and no one seemed to care. The fannish organization, which usually deferred to me on all things Witt, didn't defer this time. The fen wanted to send Witt off in style, and it didn't matter to them that the style was one he would have hated.

If I wanted to carry out Witt's matching fund wishes, then the only thing I could do was set up the world's most kickass charity auction and give it double-billing with Witt's one and *only* fannish memorial service.

I decided to hold the charity auction at the biggest West Coast science fiction convention held in that year.

The Left Coast BigCon used to be called the Megacon back in the day, but the name had been usurped by one of those corporate comic/gaming companies. The problem with the new name was BigCon wasn't really big at all, not compared with the way all of the comic conventions had grown recently. But the BigCon was the biggest sf con we had to offer on the West Coast—and I didn't dare move east. That would have been a bridge too far for the fen.

I made the auction itself an event. I pulled out all the stops, and guilted dozens of writers, artists, and old-time collector friends of Witt to donate thousands of items to the auction. Then I advertised the auction separately from, and in tandem with, the convention. I wanted big name collectors to show up, even if they weren't from the West Coast.

I billed the auction *The Wittiest, Foulest, Most Entertaining Charity Auction in the Entire Universe! Join Us To Get Your Paws on Great and Rare Things!*

And I added this in smaller font:

Memorialize our friend Witt by doing what he loved best—handling collectibles, raising money, and helping others. (His other favorite pastime, arguing for arguing's sake, will be allowed, but only outside the room.)

I figured most people would be stunned at the "helping others" phrase, because Witt kept his generosity secret. I also thought most people would laugh knowingly at the arguing part. I wanted that arguing part so that people would actually show up for Witt, not just for the collectibles.

But I was worried about attendance. That was why I let rumors start that newly located items from the estates of some of sf's great collectors —Forrest J. Ackerman's mythic Hollywood memorabilia, and Bill Trojan's spectacular book collection. We actually didn't have any of that stuff. Forry had sold off most of his collection before he died, and a lot of Trojan's collection had been sold intact to private collectors.

I expected collectors to appear because they were mercenary.

What I hadn't expected were all the people who were showing up because they were friends of Witt.

When the chair of BigCon finally approached me, asking what we were going to do with the auction—and finally got through to me about the fact that we were going to have upwards of a thousand people at the auction—we had to rent the biggest space possible from the hotel. A space big enough to put the stuff on display, and large enough to handle the gigantic crowd of collectors.

It was all last-minute, which I loathed. I'm a planner, and my planning had gone out the window.

Then the convention began, and people started pulling me aside to tell me stories about Witt.

He paid for my family's move to Arizona, said a Big Name Fan, *so I could get a good job, not the crap-ass thing I had in the Midwest.*

He paid my way through rehab, said another.

He gave me enough money to allow me and my children to flee my abusive husband, one timid writer told me.

The stories continued. One sentence here, another sentence there. Mostly whispered at me, because Witt had made each and every person promise they would tell no one.

He didn't want his largess known.

I had thought I was one of Witt's closest friends.

Turned out, I hadn't known him at all.

————

The pre-auction ceremony (read funeral) started without me. I figured staying away from the actual memorial was the least I could do to honor Witt's no-memorial-service rule.

Besides, the entire thing had morphed into a mini-convention of its own. Daniel Deggs, the con's Toastmaster and Raconteur Extraordinaire, who had been tapped as the auction's Master of Ceremonies, had even divided the day into little segments.

The first segment became the memorial service's opening ceremonies, another irony, since Witt *loathed* opening ceremonies. He had told me a thousand times that he would only attend opening ceremonies if someone had convinced him that an attractive woman would run through the room naked.

There were no naked women, but there were belly dancers, a

Washington State opening ceremonies tradition. Most of the dancers had—you guessed it—been beneficiaries of Witt's secret charitable impulses. These women wanted to dance in his memory, and dance they did.

I arrived late, but not too late for that. The Pacific Northwest fannish belly dancers were among the best in the world.

The usual suspects were there, including folks from the dealer's room who should have been tending their tables. I nearly tripped over megacollector Dwight William Weeks's wheelchair as I came in, and asked him if he wanted to move closer to the front. He shook his head. He wasn't as big a fan of the belly dancers as I was.

I stood near him in the back, arms crossed, and listened in surprise as person after person broke their oath to Witt.

Deggs started it all by giving them permission to speak.

"After all," Deggs said, as he launched into the memorial part of the memorial, "what did Witt say to all of us about his fate after death?"

What do I care? The room shouted back en masse. *I'll be dead!*

A shiver ran through me. I thought I had known Witt best of all. Had I been wrong? Had he presented that so-called secret self to everyone he helped?

"And since he's dead," Deggs said, proving this was, indeed, a fannish funeral and not the kind of carefully scripted be-nice-to-the-family funeral that happened in the mundane (non-sf) world, "let's talk honestly about Witt."

What a gamble. Because Witt had viciously insulted pretty much everyone in science fiction.

Person after person got up, walked down an incredibly long aisle, and grabbed the microphone from Deggs. Every single person described an epic verbal battle they had had with Witt, why they had thought Witt was an utter asshole back when they met him, and then they'd tell a story of generosity.

Almost every story ended with *And he told me not to tell anyone, because he didn't want his reputation ruined.*

"This would have made him so mad," Dwight muttered.

"Yeah," I said. Witt really had never wanted anyone to praise him. He wasn't that kind of man. Gratitude made him nervous.

But Dwight and I seemed to be the only grumpy souls in the room.

No one looked at the collectibles, which lined the walls. Some of the art glittered, because I had put special lighting near it. Other, more delicate valuable things, sat in shaded areas on the sides, so that light wouldn't destroy them.

I looked at the hundreds of items we had to get through. We were nearly an hour behind schedule, and we had been pushing the timeline from the beginning.

I glanced at Deggs, hoping he felt the time pressure too. The man's face was slightly red, and, as I watched, he surreptitiously raised his right hand, leaned his head toward it, and wiped underneath his right eye with his thumb.

Good heavens, he was crying. Had Witt done him a kindness too?

If so, this Witt love-fest would never end.

My heart was hammering in my chest. I pushed off the wall I'd been leaning on, and walked up the side aisle, past the memorabilia from the first *Star Wars* movie back in 1977, past the collectables from the original *Star Trek* TV series, past the key issues of several Marvel comics, ready for bids. Deggs saw me, and tried to shake me off, but I was channeling Witt.

We only had this room until midnight, and I had done the math. I figured it would take at least eight hours to go through all this stuff, and then there would be the two hours (minimum) we needed for payment and organization. Yeah, we could do some of it on Sunday, but not all of it. We were on the clock.

Then a hand grabbed my arm. I looked down to see Paladin

standing next to me. Her eyes were clear, but her eyelashes were spikey as if moisture had stuck them together.

I tried to make that compute. Paladin was here? And she had teared up? Both things, I figured, were next to impossible.

I had known Paladin for years now. She and I had worked cases together, and I'm pretty sure she saved my life once.

Even with all of that, I don't know Paladin's real name. She's managed to keep it from me—rather like Witt kept all of his acts of generosity from me.

"I need to talk to you," Paladin said in a quiet voice.

She looked tired, something I'd never quite seen before. Paladin is small and strong. Sometimes I think she's a pixie or a member of the fae. She's the only person I know in real life (not in fannish makeup) who has real God-given pointed ears.

Normally, I would have done anything Paladin asked, but we were on the clock—

"*Now*," she said, in a not-so-quiet voice.

Then she herded me through a side door that led into the kitchen area, a door I had insisted on keeping locked, so that the collectibles would stay safe. The fact that the door was unlocked caught my attention almost as much as the determination on Paladin's face.

In the fluorescent light, I saw that she was wearing her signature black T-shirt and black jeans. Only, for once, her T-shirt did not have an image or a message. She was wearing black, as in mourning clothes.

As in funeral clothes.

Which meant that she too had known Witt.

How did I not know that?

"This thing is running behind," I said.

"Good," she said, "because we have a problem."

I frowned at her, resisting the urge to glance at the door. "What is it?"

"The fanzines are gone," she said.

The fanzines, mimeographed and mailed to fen all over the world, had kept sf fandom alive in the era before the internet. The fanzines were amateur magazines that sometimes had followings as big as the prozines (the regular magazines).

The collection of fanzines we had at this auction was truly special. We had rare, famous and hard-to-find issues of fanzines that some had believed only existed in fannish lore. We had several issues of *Stymie*, written and published by the late film critic Roger Ebert when he was still a kid in school. We had the first issue of what most believe to be the first fanzine, *Comet*, published in 1930, and signed by both of its creators, Raymond Palmer and Walter Dennis. We had all five issues of *Science Fiction*, the 1933 fanzine edited by Jerry Siegel who (with Joe Shuster) went on to create Superman, which we were selling as a lot.

We had the tenth issue of OSFAN, published in 1970, prized because it marked the first publication of the notorious *Eye of Argon*, written by a sixteen-year-old Jim Theis. The story was well known, not because it was good, but because it was famously bad, and the fen had adopted reading it aloud as a party game.

My favorite donation, though, and the one that had generated the most interest was the legendary thirteenth issue of *Goop, Grope, and Grimm*, published on Halloween, 1963. It contained "The Adventures of Morgana Jones," the most famous piece of fan fiction ever written. The story predicted Kennedy's assassination less than a month away, at Dallas, in a school bookstore (close enough), as well as the rise of *Star Trek*, which the story had called *Wagon Train in Space*. Coincidentally (or not), that title was how Roddenberry pitched the show to the Hollywood suits.

Arguments in fannish circles debated whether the author, the pseudonymous Walter Waltine Waltette (or W[3] as he became known), was actually psychic or friends with both Lee Harvey

Oswald and Gene Roddenberry—which seemed to me to be highly improbable, although not as improbable as the other theories as to why the story was so chockful of future lore. Some believed a time traveler wrote it; others simply claimed the fanzine had the wrong date on the cover and had actually appeared in 1968 not 1963. Other fen claimed they had received their copy in early November 1963, and had been shocked at the ties to the Kennedy assassination.

However, no one in the government had ever investigated W^3, at least as far as we knew, although the House Select Committee on Assassinations talked to a variety of fen in 1977, trying to track down W^3, to see what he knew. Not even the editor/publisher of *Goop, Grope, and Grimm*, Ike Gopnik, knew him. Ike claimed under oath before Congress that the story had shown up on his doorstep in early July 1963, and he thought it cool, so he published it.

Ike had dined out on his moment in the Congressional spotlight for another decade, before he went to the Great Convention in the Sky. However, the issue of *Goop, Grope, and Grimm*, like a lot of other things in this auction, had come from his private collection.

That collection had been rescued—quite literally—from a Dumpster by a Big Name Fan who shall remain nameless for the purposes of this tale. Now that fan was getting up there, and he was divesting himself of the parts of his collection he knew he would never look at again.

The fanzine collection had been the most complete collection I had ever seen. I had heard, from the fannish grapevine, that no one had seen a collection like it. There were gems in those mimeographed sheets that most of us had believed to be creations of fannish lore, not actual fanzines themselves.

"What do you mean the fanzines are gone?" I asked Paladin.

"Stolen," she said softly.

"How is that even possible?" I asked.

She leaned back and raised her eyebrow, Spock-like. Paladin had taken that signature move from classic Trek and had turned it into a look filled with such disdain that nothing else I had ever seen rivaled it.

"I'm assuming they came in with a few boxes, packed up the fanzines, and walked out," she said. "Through this unlocked door."

I blushed. I often blush around Paladin. She unnerves me in a variety of ways.

"I didn't mean how did they steal it," I said, "although, come to think of it, that's a good question. We theoretically had state-of-the-art security here."

She started to respond, but I talked over her.

"I mean," I said, "how come you know about this and no one had bothered to tell me? I'm supposed to be running this show after all."

I sounded petulant. I hadn't meant to sound petulant, but I was. And a little worried. The Big Name Fan had entrusted us with his precious collection, and was monitoring the auction from his home in Texas. He and I both expected the fanzines to sell for nearly $200,000 all by themselves. After all, this was the perfect audience to overspend on famous fanzines. Or infamous fanzines. Or, rather, tiny mimeographed collectibles that no one outside our fannish family would give a rat's ass about.

"I'm telling you now," Paladin said in her most no-nonsense voice. That voice told me she was on the job. Which meant that the convention had hired her (*hired* her!) to find the fanzines, because they didn't want me to know about the theft.

Paladin wasn't well known for recovering stolen items at conventions. She called herself a bulldozer. She specialized in finding kidnap victims or saving kids from pedophiles or secreting abused family members out of truly bad situations.

Which, come to think of it, was probably how Paladin had known Witt. She had probably partnered with him on many of the rescues being recounted in the gigantic function space behind us.

"How long have the fanzines been gone?" I asked.

Paladin's eyes narrowed. She took her job very seriously. I would never be able to get the details of this hire out of her, unless someone fessed up to me later.

"Paladin," I said. "I need to know. We advertised those fanzines."

As if that was the worst thing. It wasn't. There were dozens of other worst things that I was already making up.

"They were in place when the doors opened this morning," she said.

She was right. I would have noticed if they had vanished. I had done a very slow walk-through before the doors opened, eyeballing everything, although my eyeballs were a bit dry and sleep-deprived. I had been up until 4 a.m. the night before, setting everything up, and even with that I'd been too wired to sleep. So my eagle-eyes had probably been less eagle and more mole-like.

"So the fanzines were taken while people were here?" I asked, trying to make that compute. I hadn't arrived with the crowds, I hadn't seen how they had chosen their seats, I hadn't seen what Deggs had done from the start.

I also hadn't checked the doors around the room, like the one Paladin and I had just gone through.

"I don't know," Paladin said. "We have security footage, but that part of the room is dark."

It wasn't dark. It was dim. And I had set it up that way because I didn't want the artificial lighting to ruin the fanzines, some of which hadn't seen daylight in nearly fifty years. Deggs had complained. He had said that people needed to see the items clearly.

But he had complained about the fact that the fen attending couldn't pick up the fanzines and thumb through them. The very idea made me shudder. What if someone creased a page? Made a micro-tear? Deggs had run dozens of auctions, but he clearly wasn't a collector. A tiny crease in a page could cost us hundreds, by bringing down the price.

That was why I had insisted on keeping the fanzines, as well as the comics and other truly valuable paper collectibles, in cases. No one could touch them, except the organizers. And I, personally, had bought each and every person working this auction their own pair of gloves for handling the material.

I also put cotton glove boxes, filled to the brim with the cheap gloves that you sometimes found in libraries, so that no one would get their sweaty, chocolate-covered fingers on any of the collectibles. Anyone who wanted to touch *anything* had to put on a glove first.

Yes, I had said to Deggs when he complained about that too, I knew it wasn't common at convention auctions. But this was Witt's auction with some truly high-end collectibles, and I wanted to make sure we did it right.

"Which security footage were you using?" I asked.

"What do you mean, which security footage?" Paladin asked.

I closed my eyes just for a half-second. They were so tired, they wanted to stay closed. I didn't blame them. I was weary— first from handling Witt's estate along with my own work, and from this auction.

I opened my eyes to see Paladin staring at me, a crease in her forehead. I liked to think that crease was concern for me, but it might simply have been her puzzling over the security footage.

"They should have brought you in right from the start," she said, the crease getting deeper. "I told them that."

An exhausted anger flared in me. I almost lashed out, but I

knew this wasn't Paladin's fault. I'd be talking to the convention organizers when this was all over.

"Why didn't they?" I asked.

She tilted her head a little. Her mouth opened, then closed, and then that crease turned into a full-blown frown.

"I, um…They…um…" She shook her head slightly. Paladin was not good at subtle. And she couldn't finesse anything. "Ah, hell. I hear you've been a bit difficult lately, Spade."

Difficult? *I* had been difficult? *Me?* With all the organizing and the work and the crap I had to do to get Witt's estate in order, the people fighting me on every turn, *I* had been the difficult one? *Me?*

I started to say all of that and then actually heard it. In my head. Actually heard it. The clear definition of difficult. I usually worked well with others. I didn't fly off the handle. I didn't use my sharp tongue as a weapon the way Witt had. I rarely attacked anyone, unless attacked first.

"Point taken," I said.

She raised her eyebrows just a bit. Apparently she had seen my mental change of course.

I needed to get my ego out of all of this and get to work. Fast.

"When and how did they bring you in?" I asked.

"About an hour into the memorial," Paladin said. "I was standing in the back and they pulled me into the hallway."

About an hour in. Fifteen minutes before I showed up.

"Were the belly dancers in the hallway out front here?" I asked.

"No," she said. "They were waiting in the kitchen."

Then she made a face as she realized that this door had been unlocked right from the start. And probably unlocked by the very people I had tasked with keeping it locked at all times.

It was my own fault. I had trusted the convention committee with a lot of this stuff, rather than the usual security team. I had worked the security team to death in the days before the convention, guarding the shipments, making sure that someone was at the door at all times.

Which meant that whoever had taken the fanzines had known that the A team had guarded the stuff *before* the auction started. The question was, had they known it because this was a so-called inside job or because they had walked the hallway and tried to get in from the start.

"You thought of something," Paladin said, as if that was a surprise.

I had thought of a lot of somethings, none of which I was ready to share.

"I need my computers and all the security footage you can find," I said to her.

"Where will you be?" she asked.

I wanted to be in the room, monitoring the auction, but I needed my Tower of Terror.

"Con Ops," I said, and headed that way.

No matter what convention I was at, Con Ops—convention operations—always smelled the same by Saturday. A combination of old pizza, spilled soda, and dirty feet. By Sunday, throw in some gamer-level B.O. and a hint of rotting bananas, and you had the stench that would take Con Ops to the Dead Dog party and beyond.

No one worked Con Ops for the entire convention straight. A rotating compliment of SMoFs (Secret Masters of Fandom) and local fen moved in and out of the room, constantly doing their jobs and overseeing everything they possibly could. At this moment, only three people sat in Con Ops, buried deeply in some work particular to them.

Usually, I lived in Con Ops during any convention I was a part of, but this BigCon wasn't usual. I had never been so deeply involved in a charity auction before, and I hoped I would never be again.

Still, I had set up my Tower of Terror in its usual spot on the side of the very large room. My computer system, which had only grown larger and more elaborate as most people's computers had grown smaller, looked intimidating. It should: I had encryption hardware on it that rivaled the best Silicon Valley firms. In fact, I had consulted at more than a few of them, and helped them with their designs, particularly for their financial protocols.

In front of the Tower of Terror sat my chair. No one but me touched my chair. My chair had more buttons and levers than a Navy destroyer. And it was set up to my specifications, so on that level, I would know if someone monkeyed with it.

Although there was one person known to monkey with it—and that was Paladin.

I sat down gingerly, just in case she had changed something. But she hadn't. Then I grabbed three laptops. I had placed several hidden cameras near all the collectibles. I had also placed several visible cameras around the auction. The visible camera feed ran to a small laptop that I kept in the auction room, as well as to the cloud so that I could access them from anywhere.

I had wanted people to know they were being watched. But I also wanted them to relax a little, and to believe that those visible cameras were the *only* cameras.

The hidden cameras fed into one of my clean laptops. There was nothing else on that laptop. I grabbed it and rewound the feeds on that too. If I needed to, I would combine the hidden and the visible camera feeds on a third laptop and see what it told me.

I focused on the visible cameras first. I studied the area near the fanzines. Yeah, it was dark, but I had set up two different kinds of visible cameras there—a regular one and an infrared. I moved the imagery from the regular camera forward slow enough that I could see everything, but not so slowly that it ran in real time.

Sure enough, about twenty minutes into the memorial, someone dropped a white glove over the camera itself. I reversed the image and slowed it down, going frame by frame, hoping to see whoever had done this. But no one appeared.

Whoever had done it had known how to stay out of camera range.

Once I determined that I couldn't see the person from the visible camera, I fast forwarded quickly, waiting until someone peeled the glove off the camera. That had come forty-five minutes in when a member of the concom discovered the missing fanzines.

I let out a soft whistle, annoyed that it had been so very easy. Then I went back and watched the imagery of the glove covering the camera again. There was no hand, nothing, no sideways shot of flesh or a fingernail or anything. Not even any movement.

So, I rewound the infrared to that exact moment, and compared frame by frame. I saw a lot of movement far away, but no heat signature close enough to drop that glove over the camera.

That irritated me.

So I got up, grabbed a Coke, stared at the untouched veggie platters on the snack table, and grabbed cheese and crackers instead. I hoped I wouldn't be here long enough to regret failing to order a pizza.

I ate the cheese and crackers quickly, cleaned off my hands, and then went back to work, dragging my Coke with me. I didn't sip it though. I stared at it for a moment, thinking about Witt's death. Then I set the unopened Coke back in the bucket of ice, and pulled out a bottle of water instead.

Small steps. Small, small steps.

I returned to my chair, and opened the other laptop. This time I examined the footage from all the hidden cameras. I started with the cameras closest to the fanzines. None were really close to the fanzines. I figured no one would want to steal those. My mistake.

No one dropped any gloves or coverings on the hidden cameras. Apparently, no one had seen them, which was as I intended.

I watched, but couldn't see anyone near the table at all as the glove fell onto the visible camera.

Then I reversed the footage from the hidden cameras. Yep, I got four different views of that glove floating onto the table, but none of anyone standing *in front of* the table.

I cursed in Klingon.

At that moment, Paladin entered Con Ops with a flash drive in her hand.

"Hotel security," she said. "Including some stuff they didn't want to hand over."

Then she gave me a feral little smile. I was glad I hadn't been in the room with her when she got this.

I took the flash drive, and opened one of the air-gapped laptops. I didn't want any virus or program leaching into my systems or into the systems for Con Ops. I'd learned the hard way that hotel systems, particularly those of hotels at various science fiction and comic conventions, had some of the most creative viruses.

There were four hotel security cameras in that large auction room, because that room had initially been four large ballrooms. Usually they were separated by walls that the hotel could break down for bigger groups. No one noticed those walls, not even in their absence. One camera for one room.

But I didn't want to see the images from those four cameras.

Not yet anyway. As I was downloading the footage onto the air-gapped laptop, I went to the one with the visible cameras and opened the security footage from one of the cameras faraway, a camera that faced the fanzines.

On that footage, they looked dark. I had set up the cameras before I laid out the items up for bid, so I went all the way back to the beginning of the footage, days ago, when the only people in the hotel had been me and the concom.

"Who're you looking for?" Paladin asked, startling me. I had forgotten she was there.

It wasn't often I forgot Paladin. She wasn't the forgettable type. But I'd been so wrapped up in my work...

"I'm checking my memory," I said, not answering her directly.

Finally, I got to the moment after the cameras were set up. The tables were in place, but the chairs weren't. Some of the hotel staff was putting them out. The bang-slap of metal chairs being opened echoed throughout the footage.

I zoomed in as much as I could on the empty table with its standard issue hotel table cloth. Black, like we had requested, because black showed off the goods better than almost any other color. And it didn't reflect the light.

I wasn't looking at the table or the cloths, though. Nor was I looking at the people.

I was staring at that back wall.

It wasn't a wall. It was a collapsible wall.

Which surprised me just a little, because we hadn't been given the option of expanding lengthwise. We were able to open between the various rooms—width wise—but not the back.

"What's behind that wall?" I asked Paladin.

"Nothing," she said.

"Something," I said. "That wall's one of the collapsible ones."

"Only there, though," she said. "Look."

Her fingertip touched the imagery. She was right. The

collapsible wall only ran the length of that particular ballroom—one of the side ballrooms, as far from the kitchen as possible.

"Do we have footage from behind that so-called wall?" I asked.

"Not that I saw," she said.

"Would you do a walk-around for me?" I asked.

"A what?" she asked.

"Get hotel security to take you back there, and see whatever it is that's behind that wall."

"Spade," she said in a cautious tone. "Hotel security doesn't like me very much right now."

"Can you do this computer work?" I asked.

"I don't even know what *this computer work* is," she said.

I nodded. I knew she didn't.

"Then, Obiwan," I said, "you are our only hope."

She glared at me. "You don't look like Princess Leia." she said half under her breath.

"Then I'm in good company," I said. "Because Carrie Fisher doesn't look like her either."

Paladin gave me one of those looks, the one that suggested I had crossed some kind of line.

"I prefer General Leia Organa," she said.

"I prefer solving this before the thief has too much of a head start on us," I said, turning my chair so that I could urge her to get out of the room.

But she was already gone.

———

I got lost in footage, ghost images, and infrared visions. Normally, I would have combined all of the footage into one gigantic masterpiece, but I didn't have time. Besides, I didn't want to merge files that could end up compromising each other.

Fen knew a lot about computers, and I was just paranoid enough to worry that the theft of the fanzines was the kind of thing that someone would use to set me up and load a virus on my Tower of Terror. After all, that someone had to know that I would be involved. They also had to know that I would use hotel security camera footage to find the thief.

And they might know that the footage could be downloaded on a flash drive with tons of memory. They might think I was incautious enough to insert a strange flash drive into the Tower of Terror.

They, of course, would be wrong.

I had so many little screens open on my laptop screen that I wondered if this was what a fly felt like, viewing all kinds of things at once. I had learned how to process that much information coming at me at one time, and most of it didn't even register.

So when I saw the darkness around the fanzines grow on several of my security feeds, I didn't discount it as a glitch. Instead, I slowed the relevant feeds down, used a program in some video software to see if anything had changed in the recording (it hadn't), and then looked to see what exactly had changed.

Some of the small lights I had installed far from the fanzines, but close enough to add to the ambient light, had shut off.

Deliberate, and traceable.

I made a mental note, and continued viewing the footage. Something moved ever so slightly behind the table. I caught that on several feeds as well.

Then the glove floated down from the back, its whiteness catching the light.

I wondered how people missed this, so I brought up the sound on one of the camera feeds—and recognized the voice that was speaking.

It belonged to aging pin-up girl, Delilah Danvers, whose

entire career had been about her looks and her…um…assets. The fen kept her alive, going from convention to convention, auto-graphing 1950s cheesecake photos, and all of the art that she had inspired. She was famous in fandom, but not really famous anywhere else, not any more.

And she was sobbing her way through a story about Witt. Seemed he had helped her too, keeping her house from being foreclosed and inviting her to her first convention in 1980 or so, starting the revival of her "pin-up" career.

I realized, as I was startled by her voice, that I hadn't been watching the feed either. I had been listening to that incredibly riveting tale. I rewound the footage, not liking the idea that had come to me, that Delilah was somehow involved in this.

The woman who had sobbed like that wouldn't have been willing to steal from the auction, would she?

I accidentally rewound that footage too far, and hit *start* (yeah, okay, she got to me), and another voice—this one belonging to Groot, a SMoF friend of mine—shook and broke as he recounted the way that Witt had gotten Groot to the hospital and paid for his care after he was nearly beaten to death by some anti-gay bigots in the 1990s.

Okay. That stopped me too. It wasn't that Groot or Delilah were involved in the theft. It was the memorial itself. The thief either took advantage of the heartrending stories as a spur of the moment thing or the thief had gambled that people would be too upset to notice.

Or maybe he simply thought that no one would care about the fanzines. I had certainly thought so, or I would have put more protection around them. I had them there for a specific kind of collector. I hadn't expected the general public to be interested.

I moved the footage forward to that moment where the lights went dim and went frame by frame in several different security feeds. In one, I finally saw what I had been looking for.

The back wall didn't just fold back. It was composed of large square panels. Apparently they could be removed too, because one slid out of the way. A black-clad arm ending in a fist emerged from the back. The fist almost reached the visible cameras when it opened, releasing the glove. It went back and did the same thing on the other visible cameras, all within thirty seconds.

Never mind. This had been planned at least since we attached the memorial to the auction.

Once the cameras were covered, both hands emerged, along with the silhouette of a slight figure. The person quickly piled up the fanzines—the ones that were scattered in front of the visible cameras—and then eased them back. They disappeared into the opening in the wall.

Then the hands emerged one more time, grabbing the Lucite cases that held the most valuable fanzines, and sliding them into the back.

I finally understood why the lights had to be dimmed. The movement of those cases would have reflected nearby light, no matter how small, and made the move visible.

But it had barely been visible. The cases disappeared into the hole, then the panel went back into place.

The fanzines were gone—and it had taken less than three minutes.

"Wow," I said, impressed in spite of myself. If this wasn't a professional job, then it was the closest thing I had ever seen.

Which made my stomach knot up. Because I had no idea how we were going to catch a professional thief of this quality.

Then "The Ballad of Paladin" blared in Con Ops.

I picked up my cell phone with shaking hands. "Yeah?" I said.

"Good job, Spade," Paladin said. "We found the fanzines."

I blinked, going from despair to confusion in one quick second. "What?"

"They were exactly where you said they'd be," she said. "In the back behind the wall. You want me to put them back out?"

I was so confused I almost said yes. But something was wrong here. Why pull the fanzines back and not take them away? To store for later, so they could be easily removed under cover of darkness? But wouldn't it have been better to move them when no one knew they were gone?

This wasn't making sense to me.

"I'll be right there," I said, as I hung up and tucked the cell in my pocket.

———

The back area behind the fanzine table was smaller than I expected. There was barely enough room for me, the fanzines, and Paladin. A hotel security guard stood just outside, shifting from foot to foot as he waited for us.

Apparently, this hotel had been through a new remodel each time it got new owners—and it had had new owners ten times in the last fifteen years. This space was clearly supposed to be storage, but it had gotten blocked by metal kitchen shelves.

Paladin had showed me the fingerprints in the dust and dirt, where someone had moved the shelving unit to reveal this dark space. I was leery of all of it, considering the spider webs and the centuries of dirt. Someone had to have known that this space was here in order to use it. There was no way anyone would have stumbled on it.

Paladin was using a gigantic square flashlight, the kind police organizations used to illuminate big unlit spaces. I had no idea where she got it. It revealed even more dirt and grime, and a cleared-out area where the boxes were.

It also revealed handprints—or rather, glove prints—on a

bunch of the fake wall panels. Apparently our Bad Guy had tried several of the panels to see if they worked.

Which meant that he (she?) had to have been here before, at least once, to know where everything was.

As I suppressed a sneeze at all the dust, I tried to remember when we designed the layout for all of the auction goods. Donations had continued to arrive as late as Wednesday, and all of them were really good. I had moved things around several times before Thursday morning.

I had had a lot of help, as well, most of it from volunteers and other SMoFs.

"Problem solved, right, Spade?" Paladin asked again. She glanced at the wall between us and the auction. I could hear Deggs' auction patter. It sounded like he was moving quickly.

"This is weird," I said, and put out a hand for the flashlight. She gave it to me. I inspected all parts of the back area. There were prints here, but I would wager they were glove prints, not handprints. And they were small.

Still, we had the fanzines back. I glanced at my phone. We were thirty minutes from the first break in the auction itself. We had several scheduled, with meals nearby. We couldn't work Deggs for twelve hours straight, but he wanted to handle the auction alone. So we had twenty-minute breaks built in, with food carts in the hallway at the ready.

"Let's get these zines out of here," I said. I wanted the fanzines in good light, to make sure that they weren't covered with dirt or ruined.

Paladin got some boxes from the storage area and put towels in the bottom without me even asking. She also brought me gloves, which I wouldn't have thought of until I bent over near the fanzines.

I slipped on the gloves and picked up the first stack of fanzines. I was worried that all this mishandling had ruined the bottom fanzine—that it was on a bare concrete floor, covered in dirt—but I should have known better. Someone had set down fresh wood strips, then covered them with pristine white sheets.

In my CSI TV imagination—which was all I had, since I was a forensic accountant, not a forensic tech—I figured some police department could trace the wood, the sheets, and maybe even those tiny handprints.

But none of that was my concern at the moment. My concern was the fanzines. I gingerly put them in the boxes that Paladin provided. Then I sent her for some extra Lucite protective cases. I knew we had emptied out a few in the course of the auction already. The old Lucite cases would remain here, in case I got a last minute urge to call the actual police.

We finally got everything packed. My back ached and I was covered in grime. Before I unpacked the fanzines, I would have to change clothes, although I knew that would be tough. I had barely fifteen minutes to get to my room, shower and put on grime-free clothing.

Somehow I made it, even though my back ached and demanded that I stay in the hot shower longer. I didn't listen. I changed into a SMoFcon T-shirt, some black jeans, and the only other pair of shoes that I had, and still made it back to the kitchen with three minutes to spare.

Paladin remained, covered in dirt and spider webs, sitting near the boxes like the fierce warrior she was.

"What are we doing next?" she asked.

"I'm carrying these into the function space and putting them out," I said. "You're getting kitchen and storage footage from hotel security from the past week. Also, see if they'll cough up the names of any current or past employees who knew about that room."

She blew a strand of hair off her forehead, and managed to dislodge a bit of spiderweb as well.

"You act like I made friends with the security staff," she said.

I smiled for the first time since she had told me about the theft. "Just tell them that if we don't figure out who did this, they'll be on the hook for hundreds of thousands in damages."

"What damages?" she asked. "We recovered everything."

"But we have no idea what condition it's in," I said. And that was half truthful. I wanted to be the one to put the fanzines back out because I wanted to see if any of them were ruined.

Behind the door, I heard the scraping of chairs and the sound of voices. Apparently Deggs had called the break.

"See you in fifteen," I said to her as I grabbed the nearest box.

I hoped fifteen was all I was going to need.

————

Half the concom, it seemed, wanted to help me put the fanzines back out. I sent them on their way. The only person I would have trusted to help me was Deggs and he was getting a bowl of the hotel's special Pho Ga, so that his throat would remain lubricated for the next several hours of work.

I put out the loose fanzines, shaking them gently just a bit in case dirt had fallen on them. I didn't inspect as closely as I normally would have, but they seemed fine.

Then I adjusted the fanzines in the Lucite cases. I finished with five minutes to spare. And looked at the nearest case.

Something was a little off. I had set up those cases in the first place, and there had been an even number of fanzines inside of each case. In the case nearest to me, there was an odd number of fanzines.

I felt my heart sink. I took my phone out of my pocket and scanned the fanzine list I had stored on it, comparing the truly valuable ones to the ones in the case.

Sure enough, one was missing. The thirteenth issue of *Goop*,

Grope, and Grimm. I felt a little chill as I thought about the implications of that.

The room was growing louder. I turned around, scanning for Deggs. He had returned, carrying a bottle of some sports drink, which he (correctly) placed beneath his podium. Then he wiped off his hands and walked over to me.

"Well?" he asked.

"Save the fanzines until after the next break," I said to him. "I want to make sure they're laid out properly."

"Just glad we got them back," he said.

"Me, too," I said. I stayed near the table as he got the auction back under way.

I scanned the crowd. A sea of familiar faces, and some not so familiar ones. Plus a lot of familiar names, who looked a lot older than they should have. The graying of the fen commenced apace.

I was pretty convinced that the person who had stolen the fanzine was somewhere in this room. I also suspected that person hadn't left their chair during the theft itself.

I was looking for someone who had either worked here or run a con here back in the day. This hotel complex had long been a home for BigCon. I knew I was looking for a longtime fan, someone who would have been on any one of a dozen lists I had mailed or emailed information to.

I was also looking for someone with money—because they had hired muscle to steal the fanzine. I suspected that muscle had no idea about collectibles—except what our Bad Guy had told them—which told me that the Bad Guy didn't care about the condition of *Goop, Grope, and Grimm*, because simply grabbing it wrong could destroy it.

I listened as issue 25 of DC's *The Brave and The Bold*, which had an early incarnation of Suicide Squad, sold for a ridiculous $750. That outrageous competitive bidding was what I had hoped for when I set up this auction.

Then I slipped out of the room, and quietly made my way to Con Ops.

————

My Tower of Terror had an unofficial history of fandom inside its databases. I'd been going to conventions long before I became a Microsoft Millionaire, and I'd worked with concoms for decades.

I also understood patterns. That was why I was good with numbers.

I knew now I was looking for a fan who had to be old enough to have come to cons on his own in the early sixties, but young enough at the time to have written something as unbelievably awful as "The Adventures of Morgana Jones." The fan was probably LA or Vegas based, with a parent who had worked either in the entertainment industry or was connected to the Mob somehow—or both.

I didn't have to look hard. As I said, our people had been dying in droves of late. The fen, most of whom did not exercise and ate to excess, rarely lived to see eighty. My database of candidates was now shockingly small.

I called Paladin. She needed to go, along with hotel security, and guard the door to a room on the 35th floor. She asked why and I wouldn't tell her, not yet.

I needed to make sure my hunches were correct.

I shut down the Tower of Terror and headed back to the auction. This time, I entered from the back of the room, and scanned until I saw the person I was looking for.

Dwight had moved his wheelchair near the *Star Trek* collectibles from the original series, some of which he had donated to this very auction. Dwight had been a good and generous member of fandom, always willing to donate to an auction or spend a thousand or two at a charity event that was falling short.

I approached him from his good side. He'd lost an eye in a freak accident as a child.

"Can we talk?" I asked as I bent down so that he could hear me.

He gave me a sheepish look, then backed his electronic wheel-chair up. Together we headed into the hallway. It smelled of tacos and hotdogs and cinnamon rolls from the food trucks parked near the wall. I was hungry. Again.

But I was also focused.

"You could've just asked me for it," I said to Dwight. "I would have given you a special price. It probably would've been cheaper than stealing it."

His cheeks turned red. He bowed his head. He had lost most of his hair in the intervening years, except for a fringe around the back. He looked nothing like the man I had met at an early San Diego Comic-Con, back when the only people who attended were actual comic book fans. Back then he had been tall and thin, just like me. Now he outweighed me by at least a hundred pounds and had lost the use of his legs years ago.

He wouldn't be with us long either.

"I didn't want you to know I had it," he said.

"Why not?" I asked.

"Because," he whispered. "I was going to destroy it."

If I had been a true collector, I would have stepped back in horror. As someone who had been around collectors all my life, I still felt a deep shock.

"Why would you do that?" I asked, trying not to sound as judgmental as I felt.

"Because," he said, "it was the annotated version."

I had never heard of an annotated version. "What?"

He rubbed his left hand on the armrest of his wheelchair. His good eye actually teared up.

"Ike lied," he whispered.

It took me a moment to understand what he meant.

"In front of Congress?" I tried not to let my voice rise, but I wasn't sure I succeeded. The woman running the cinnamon bun food truck looked at us.

Dwight nodded. Then closed his eyes.

"He knew it was you?" I asked.

"Worse," Dwight said. "He knew about my dad."

His dad, William Dwight Weeks, who had been one of the first police officers on the scene at the Bugsy Siegel murder site in Beverly Hills. The elder Weeks had quit his job with the police to work security, first in Cuba, and then in Vegas, and finally, at the studios. Apparently, he had never lost his mob connections.

"I don't understand," I said.

Dwight glanced at the food truck operators, and a fan who sat on a bench nearby, reading a battered copy of *Ancillary Justice.* Dwight drove further down the hall, so that no one could hear us.

"My dad," Dwight said after he stopped the wheelchair. "He was involved. He handled Oswald."

So the rumors *were* true. "And he knew Roddenberry," I said.

"Yeah," Dwight said. "They were drinking buddies."

"So, you had prior knowledge of the assass—"

"No," Dwight said. "No. Like any good fanzine, *Goop, Grope, and Grimm* was months behind schedule. It came out in January."

"Why would you write a story like that about your dad?" I asked.

He shook his head. "I didn't. Ike and I were best friends. I had to tell somebody, and I told him, to my everlasting regret."

I frowned.

"He wrote the story, Spade. He put it in the fanzine and left it on *my* doorstep. Fortunately, I found it before my dad."

"Why would Ike do that?" I asked.

"Money," Dwight whispered. "My family had money. And Ike wanted some of it."

"He was *blackmailing* you?"

Dwight nodded. "Until my dad found out that I was giving Ike money, although he never found out why. Threatened to cut off Ike's body parts one at a time if he ever spoke to me again. Apparently, Ike didn't know Dad was dead by the time he testified before Congress."

Dwight ran a hand over his face. I had never seen him so nervous. Or so upset.

"I thought the issue was closed after Ike died," Dwight said. "Especially when I heard that Ike's family had tossed out Ike's collection. I didn't know that particular copy of *Goop, Grope, and Grimm* still existed until I got your flyer."

"Still, Dwight, I would have given it to you if you asked," I said.

"But you might have looked at it," he said.

I frowned. "What's in that issue?"

His lips thinned. "A different version," he said. "With all the details."

"Your dad's gone," I said. "Why not just turn the story over to the authorities? A lot of people wonder what really happened."

Dwight shook his head just a little. "I can't," he whispered. He seemed terrified.

"Dwight," I said. "It's been fifty-three years. Surely no one would hurt you or your family if this came out."

He bit his lower lip. Those tears still threatened.

"I can't risk it," he said.

I let out a breath. "It's in your hotel room, right?"

He grabbed my arm so tightly that he pulled the skin. "Spade, seriously. Don't pick it up. Don't touch it. Don't do anything with it. Please."

I thought about it for a moment. Who would believe an annotated version of a fanzine story from the 1960s held the key to the murder of JFK? I wasn't sure I did, even if Dwight's dad had been as mobbed up as the histories made it seem.

"Tell you what," I said. "You do two things. You tell me who you hired to grab the fanzine."

"Sure," he said a little too eagerly.

"And you pay the auction for the fanzine. Right now. No questions asked. Like you should have from the beginning."

"How much?" he asked.

I wasn't feeling as kind as I usually did. Who knew how high that thing would have gone in the bidding?

I knew what I had hoped the fanzine would bring. I named a price twice as high as that.

He looked a little pale. But his family had once had money. Maybe he still did as well.

"Okay," he said after a moment.

"Okay," I said. "But we're not done. We're going to checkout, and you're going to pay for the fanzine right then and there. Once the payment goes through, we'll give you the fanzine."

"Don't read it, Spade," he said.

I nodded, making no real promise at all.

————

I asked Paladin to photocopy the entire fanzine in the business center, and then hold onto the fanzine until Dwight's funds cleared. I had her hand me the photocopy, and she gave him the fanzine.

Which he burned in front of us.

I read the story days later. It had footnotes, and a lot of names, all of which had been in the Warren report on the assassination and were also mentioned at the House Select Committee on Assassinations.

Dwight had been blackmailed for nothing.

His dad had worked *security*, as in *security guard*, not as in one of the inner circle of any of the mobbed up groups he'd been near. From everything I could gather, with twenty-twenty hindsight, his dad had been one of those little men who tried to make himself more important than he actually was.

Although, this theory nagged at me a bit. I did some digging and never really could figure out where the family money came from.

Not that it mattered. Dwight died several months later. The thief, Rose Beetum, a young gamer who thought she was doing a live-action role with her favorite character, was banned from West Coast conventions for five years, although I suspected that wouldn't stick.

And the auction went off well enough that we were only fifty thousand short of the matching funds goal, which shocked the heck out of me. I got some Big Name Fans to put up the rest of the money, and we made a huge donation to Witt's favorite charity, marked—as per his wishes—Anonymous.

Witt would have loved it. All of it.

Intrigue, presidential conspiracy theories, collectibles. I found it fascinating that things so important to the fen—fanzines and storytelling—probably would have made no difference to investigators in the decades-old assassination saga. Maybe it would have made a difference in the 70s, though, when the people involved were still alive. But I doubt that.

Although I did mail a copy, anonymously, to the FBI, not that it mattered. The FBI had been embroiled in controversies of its own for the past year, and probably didn't have time for old conspiracies. I never heard anything from anyone.

Which probably would have pleased Witt as well.

I think about him a lot, even though I'm done with the estate. I miss him more than I thought possible.

Ever since the auction, people ask me if I have a Witt story. I always smile and say I have a lot of them. They insist, trying to probe to see if I have the kind of Witt story that everyone told at the memorial.

I do have one. It involves those dark days before I got my high-powered Microsoft job, when I thought I was alone in the world, and I had nearly lost hope.

But I had promised Witt I would never tell anyone what he did.

And I keep my promises.

Every single one of them.

In memory of Bill Trojan

"I tried to organize a stampede, but everybody has their own agenda."

ACKNOWLEDGMENTS

Thank you to the following wonderful people who supported the 2017 *Pulphouse Fiction Magazine* Kickstarter Subscription Drive.

Steve Perry
Steve Jenkins
Valerie Brook
Woelf Dietrich
Christian Wood
Michael A. Burstein
Martin Greening
Lynette Aspey
Mary Jo Rabe
Nancy Sweetland
Denise Baker Gaskins
Jim Gotaas
Paula Meengs
Amy Browning
Anders M. Ytterdahl

Tasha Turner

Darragh Metzger

Tony

Dan 'Grimmund' Long

Wulf Moon

David Macpherson

Linda Banche

Lianne

M. L. Buchman

Ken Hattaway

Sharan Volin

Ryan M. Williams

Justin Burnett

Brian D Lambert

Thomas Bull

Andreas Flögel

Marianne Villanueva

Meyari McFarland

Amadan

Linda Bruno

Maralee Nelder

Jessica Doyle

Tony Hernandez

Pierre L'Allier

B.J. Baye

John Ordover

AJ Lemke

John Devenny

Debb & O'Neil De Noux

Doug Houseman

Vera Soroka

Chuck Gatlin

C Kobayashi

Cathy Green

Kate Pavelle

Leah

Willard A. Stone

Chuck Emerson

John Lorentz & Ruth Sachter

Paul McNamee

Eric Kent Edstrom

Stephanie Lucas

Keith Garrett

Keith Beals

Kristyn Willson

Dayle Dermatis

Risa Scranton

Piet Wenings

Mark Kuhn

Kathryn Goldman

David Macfarlane

Ron Vitale

Walter Hawn

David Bruns

Diana Deverell

Lois Malby Olmstead

Rob Menaul

Sean Mead

Mary Haldeman

AnnieB

Diane Sayer

Sam McDonald

Katherine Crispin

Skevos Mavros

Danny Evarts

Kai

Jaq Greenspon

Doug Red

Sara Litt

Simo Muinonen

Lisa Silverthorne

Kathryn Hodghead

Rick Lawler

Caryl Giles

Charles Pearson

C. Kirk

Darren Eggett

Lisa Owen

Blythe Ayne

Erik T Johnson

Kate MacLeod

Lillian Csernica

Ann Kellett

J Stuart Pratt

Sam Turner

D.V. Berkom

Greg Gorden

Jeff Metzner

Nancy Johnson

Robert Clemens

Joy Oestreicher

Christina

FredH

John Rogers

Donald Mark

Gary Piserchio

Richard Boulter

Anne J

Dawn Watson

Tanith Korravai

Cassidy Percoco

Marnilo C

Vito Michienzi

Jason Zippay

Terry gene, novelist

John M. Portley

Andrew Bain

Rob Voss

Lauren Gemmell

Lee French

Luigi Ballabio

Andy

Richard Parks

Gregory Lovell

Kev Partner

M. Mahar

Allan Kaster

Angela Penrose

Jamie DeBree

J.V. Ackermann

Geoff Palmer

A.J. Abrao

Rebecca M. Senese

J.R. Murdock

Christine Connell

Ashley Pollard

Steven Rief

John Winkelman

Steve R

Bill

Leigh Saunders

Christine

AM Scott

donald crossman

Louisa Swann

Brent Bissell

Rob Vagle

Sharon Rowse

J & M Lowry

Mark Leslie

I.G. Frederick

Rick Lohmeyer

Jeff Soesbe

Michael Kowal

James Husum

Eugenia Parrish

Teri Babcock

Debbie Nulf

Sean Roach

Ken Talley

A.R. Henle

Justin Johnson

Jennifer Brinn

John Haines

Robert McCarter

Mary Kennedy

Kate Rooney

Lana Ayers

Gerard Ackerman

Jane Reeves Newell

Werner Meyer

Stefon Mears

Travis Heermann

Ray Vukcevich

Simon Horvat

Gregory Wade Stitz

Christina York

Fred A. Aiken

Anonymous Reader

Patrick

Joshua Cooper

W.A. Brown

Damien Filer

Andrew Hatchell

James Beach

Harvey Stanbrough

Sabrina Chase

Melissa H. Taylor

Paula Whitehouse

Alexandra Brandt

Joshua Maher

Annie Reed

Ranveig Wallace

Sarah C

Felicia Fredlund

Trent Walters

J. E. Hopkins

coraa

Daphne Riordan

Gary Jonas

Chris Abela

Celine Malgen

Marcelle Dubé

Sheila Watson

Chrissy Wissler

Joanna Penn

Chong Go Sunim

Johanna Rothman

Rob Slater
Laura Ware
Danica Oakley
David Hendrickson
Angie Simon
Amy Laurens
kathryn mccloskey
Linda
Mary Fishler-Fisk
Camille Lofters
Linda Maye Adams
Katrina Tipton
Kenneth Norris
Carolyn Rowland
Mark Grant
Stuart Jaffe
John Payne
Sharon Reamer
Len Chang
Robert Battle
James Wisher
Anthony St. Clair
Lena Goldfinch
Christina Martin
Marie Laura
Kari Kilgore
Derek Miller
Keith West
Emily Williams
Michael and Nitu Gulati-Pauly
Stephen Couch
Matt Herron
David Brown

Catalyst Games
Johnny Pedersen
Tracy May Adair
Joseph Wrzos
Terry Mixon
Turner L.
Lynda Foley
Fran Friel
Lisa Satterlund
Steven H Silver
Todd Goetz
Sandra Hofsommer
Bonnie S Warford
Al Harris
R.F. Kacy
Joy Johnson
Karen Shannon
Bonnie Koenig
Michael Harbour
Lyndon Perry
Scott Tefoe
Michael Nisivoccia
Christel Adina Loar
Michael La Ronn
Ashley Pollard
Steve R
Christine
Louisa Swann
Sharon Rowse
I.G. Frederick
Michael Kowal
Teri Babcock
Ken Talley

Jennifer Brinn

Mary Kennedy

Gerard Ackerman

Stefon Mears

Simon Horvat

Fred A. Aiken

Joshua Cooper

Andrew Hatchell

Sabrina Chase

Alexandra Brandt

Ranveig Wallace

Trent Walters

Daphne Riordan

Celine Malgen

Chrissy Wissler

Johanna Rothman

Danica Oakley

Amy Laurens

Mary Fishler-Fisk

Katrina Tipton

Mark Grant

Sharon Reamer

James Wisher

Christina Martin

Derek Miller

Michael and Nitu Gulati-Pauly

David Brown

Tracy May Adair

Turner L.

Lisa Satterlund

Sandra Hofsommer

www.ingramcontent.com/pod-product-compliance
Lightning Source LLC
Chambersburg PA
CBHW020653030726
47498CB00002B/490